All rights reserved. No part of this publication may be reproduced, stored in a retrieval system, in any form or by any means without the prior written permission of the author, nor be otherwise circulated in any form of binding or cover other than that in which it is published and without similar condition being imposed on the subsequent purchaser.

All characters in this book are fictitious and any resemblance to real persons, living or dead, is purely coincidental.

Copyright Altany Craik 2020

For all of my friends and family who kept on reading snippets and never complained.

Innocence Lost

by

Altany Craik

Chapter 1

As usual, the de-mister was taking a long time to clear the inner frost on my windscreen. A high pitched squeal, like a kettle boiling in the next room, wasn't irritating enough to make me switch off the fan. Tonight was the first time I had been called back to Gleninch, the town of my childhood. Sure, I had visited my sister who still lives there, but not for a few years. I had never been called back on business. Business, like most things, was slow in Gleninch.

The journey across the Forth Road Bridge, a masterful piece of engineering with near continual resurfacing work, into the Kingdom of Fife had been uneventful and the new dual carriageway meant it was less than forty minutes since I had locked my front door. I had paid the entrance fee of one pound sterling. Fife, an exclusive land, where one pays to get in. Tolls on the entry bridges from Tayside in the north and Lothian to the south; made Fife the only place one has to pay to get into. It might have been better to charge the denizens of Fife to get out.

It was now slightly after three in the morning and bloody freezing as I drove speedily along the empty road. The recently completed regional dual carriageway meant that I wouldn't need to drive through the villages that had made up the bulk of Fife's industrial heritage. The new road would take me to the New town. It was new just after the war; tired would be a better description now. The landscape looked quite nice with a blanket of frost. Darkness hid most of the details. It was probably just as well.

I had not been freezing when my vibrating, screaming phone had woken me. A brief message from the Home office and I had been summoned. No niceties either just a summons. A warm bed had been deserted in favour of a trip to St Margaret's in the Fields, whose priest was decorating the car park with his cooling body. They only call me when it's a religious matter. A murdered priest was a religious matter, apparently. So here I was. A homecoming I neither wanted nor needed. The prodigal son returns. Maybe not.

The blue strobe lights and radio chatter give an unearthly feel to even the most mundane of situations but a murder scene seems even more bizarre. Vehicles parked, in what seems like a random order, tape flapping yellow and black and sometimes red, and uniformed and plain clothes all jumbled together like a flash mob. The noise of radios and half barked orders like a hubbub before the curtain rises; now that I was here, I supposed the curtain was about to go up. Another opening of another show.

I pulled my red Nissan Sunny in to the kerbside and waited on the uniformed officer to approach. Thankfully the screeching had subsided to a little ringing noise. He was young and cold, and mist clouds erupted when he spoke. Like puff the magic dragon, no flame just steam.

"Move along, Sir. Nothing to see here." He waggled his torch hand, indicating that I should piss off. His disinterest was written all over his face. His bulky high visibility jacket clearly identifying him as in charge.

I turned off the engine and stepped out of my car. It was bloody freezing and a shiver ran through me. His face was a cross between non comprehension and incredulity as I had totally ignored him. I pressed the lock button in my key fob and a solid clunk-kitty-clunk rang out behind me. His mouth opened but I cut in.

"They are waiting for me, I believe." I spoke calmly, telling the nice policeman nothing.

"Excuse me." He tried the hard ass. All frown and forward leaning, wielding a unibrow of impressive bushiness. I am only five ten and slim with it. This would be fun. A no contest. He might need that stab vest to protect him.

"They are waiting for me officer. I am the reason you are all still waiting in the cold." I smiled pleasantly and watched the lights come on in his empty head. He was a little slow to catch the words but he was trying.

"Who's in charge and where is the body?" I asked as I walked past him. He followed like a good fellow. He didn't have any choice, really.

"Inspector Brotherton. Rear car park." He managed to splutter not knowing what to do. He stopped, a little worried about leaving his post. He let me go on alone.

He hadn't even asked for ID; he must be new. I have identification and official looking passes for what I do, and sometimes they even get checked out. It might as well read 'God Squad'. I am a servant of the Church and empowered by the state. What a combination. When it's my area, I'm in charge. Who's the Daddy?

Turning the corner of the old white church I can see Brotherton and his detectives standing around, waiting. Waiting for me. All they will know is to touch nothing until I say so. They look so miserable and unhappy; I am sure that won't change. I am not renowned for spreading sunshine on my travels. I have difficulty making a good impression and even more difficulty giving a shit about it.

"Inspector Brotherton? Father Andrew Steel." I smile as I introduce myself, he takes the proffered hand and shakes it. No games just a handshake. I don't look much like a priest. I'm a bit untidy, I don't wear robes, need a shave and in the middle of the night my hair sticks up at the back. A combination that is guaranteed to earn instant respect and cooperation, obviously.

"Glad you could make it Father," not a trace of sarcasm, "the body is just over here." He motions onwards and starts to lead the way.

"Have you taken photos?" I expect they will have but always better to ask. He nods allowing me to pass him and go first as we get closer. Brotherton didn't seem too keen to go near. It is always this way when the body is a Priest, I don't know why that should be. A body is a body, isn't it?

Oh well, time to do my Thing. My Thing is like a gift from God, only much less impressive. I get impressions from things. I usually touch them and see what I see; I have always been able to do it. If the supernatural is involved I can feel it. If the priest was simply battered to death by a thug, then I could leave this one and go back to bed.

I was hoping for bed, most often the outcome is negative and the Police handle it. The body, I don't want the name, is face down in a pool of blood. The pool seems to emanate from the head area, like a big treacle circle. I'm going to have to move the body a little to see the wound. Wearing my long dark overcoat was a bad choice. It would get dipped in the pool of blood unless I took it off. So off it came and the sub-zero temperature caressed my back like the hand from Hell. Now I understood why it gets called the wind chill factor, all heat almost instantly blown from my skin. I handed the coat to Brotherton and squatted by the corpse. My knees protest a little but I manage not to groan like a creaking gate.

I teased the grey shot hair back from the forehead hoping I could see a bit of the face. I couldn't so I rolled him over, away from the pool. I've been splashed a few times; experience is a great teacher. I try to keep my face neutral as I see the front view, wouldn't want the provincial cops to think I was a rookie at this. I have seen a few interesting bodies.

It was not pretty, a head wound above his right eye had been the cause of death. Well his skull had been bashed in killing him pretty quickly I would expect. Bludgeoned sums it up pretty well, but I'm not the pathologist. Sometimes I wish I could just look at bodies and use my Gift. I can't, so, I have to touch. I pull in some of the chilled night time air and resist the urge to cough as my lungs protest. I don't smoke but sometimes the cough sounds so similar.

Dead bodies have a feel all of their own. Like cold feet but worse, much worse. Clammy and almost like raw chicken that has been lurking at the back of the fridge. I was chittering a bit as the wind drove the last of the heat from me. I was well and truly wind chilled. I decided the hand would be better than touching the head. I took his right hand gently and hoped for nothing. When my gift kicks in it can be a bit uncontrolled. Tonight was totally uncontrolled; I got a jolt like an electric shock. I dropped the hand like it had grown spikes and promptly fell from my squat onto my ass. Shit. I missed, by a few inches, the pool of blood. Last thing I needed was a blood stained ass. It was so undignified and credibility destroying.

"I'm sorry Inspector I'll be staying a while with this one." I extended my hand and he helped me to my feet. Not a happy look on his face and he barely knows me. I really wanted my coat, but I appreciated the help. I was still puffing a bit as I tried to catch my breath and buttoning up the coat with the fiddly buttons was a trial but I managed. The shivering becoming severe until I stuffed my hands deep in my pockets. I am aware that they are are watching expectantly.

"I need to look inside the church. Is it locked?" God squad efficiency coming to the fore. I really wanted a coffee. However out of the wind would be a start. I should really work on small talk but tonight, like most nights, I didn't make the effort.

"Can we process the body?" Someone behind me asked. I nodded, nothing to see that couldn't wait. They asked so nicely. The crew springing to life behind me was efficient looking and very little chit chat filled the night.

"The church is open, Father." Inspector Brotherton led the

way back round. The houses that overlooked St Margaret's had poltergeists twitching the curtains. One or two hardy souls stood in their doorways looking across at us as we crossed the threshold. I almost waved. That's me, the celebrity. Where were the paparazzi when you needed them? What did they expect to see? I wondered if they knew the Priest well.

It was dark inside the doorway, like the mouth of Hell, dark and gaping. I never feel afraid entering a house of God. I always feel safe, whether the lights are on or not. God lives there and we should always remember that. Brotherton didn't feel the same as he fumbled around for the light switch. He managed not to panic but he certainly wasn't comfortable. I wondered if he was scarred by early Sunday school stories or teenage horror movie experiences. Might be both.

A solid clunk and the lobby basked in a clean white light, so bright our eyes squinted in self defence. The worn red carpet showing signs of where the congregation walked, the pile flat in the middle and like new at the edges. To the right the doors into the Church itself were closed. I opened one and stepped in. The light of Christ burned steadily in its holder. God was here. So was I. No comparison really.

Why I was here was a question beyond me. The jolt from the dead priest outside called for my continued presence. Supernatural bludgeoning? I didn't think so. Traces lead to questions that lead to more questions. I was going to wander through the church and see what that turned up. Scientific method or what?

"Father." Brotherton called me back to the present. He has a deep manly voice, lucky bastard. Although he still didn't sound comfortable.

"Yes?" I'm still not that with it. I am bloody freezing. He seems to expect me to be doing something. Perhaps if I had waved a crucifix around or chanted he might have been more impressed.

"I'll get uniform to cordon off the area and place men for the rest of the night and tomorrow." His voice was almost steady. Not the religious type. No, definitely not. He had barely finished his statement and the door closed behind him. He might be tall, dark and have a manly voice but he was behaving like a chicken.

I sat my ass down on the front pew, waiting for some inspiration. Modern churches are much more informal, and it doesn't often feel that spiritual to sit in one. I prefer the old style with high stained glass windows and stone. I let my eyes wander around the church picking out the mandatory elements. I looked at the rail and wondered 'What was going on here?' New Town Scotland, with drink and drugs all around. A precinctular heaven, designed and built for modern living in the fifties. Now it was a bloody soulless dormitory town near to arterial roads and a daily massed exodus to jobs somewhere else. Town and country planners had pretty much failed to deliver on their vision. Now something else was going to blight the lives of the poor sods that lived here.

I let out a slow puff of air to see if it misted. It did. I'd be better off in the car. After a heartfelt sigh I put on my 'Best get on with it' face. Start with the obvious, the rooms at the back, after that, the office and lastly the house of God. I was hoping that I got no more impressions so I could get a place to sleep and get warm. I hate being cold, it makes me cranky. Or should I say crankier?

I hate surprises, too. Christmas presents are always opened early and I don't remember the last Birthday present that I got. Poor me. My life has been a series of little disappointments that have left me a soured middle aged grumpy man. My face was beginning to show it too.

I wandered up the red carpeted hall and felt like visiting royalty. The corridor echoed under my feet as I walked into the darker recesses of this church. The Office was a picture of efficiency. Everything had been filed correctly and not a thing was out of place. No letters in the 'in' tray, no pending items and nothing to go out either. In fact it was the most sterile Priest's office I had ever been in and I've seen lots of them. I wasn't so cold now and my brain was beginning to work; well sort of.

"What are you hiding? Come on, what is it?" I speak to myself, often. Usually its drivel but sometimes I amaze myself. I looked under the desk and slid my hand across the dark floor. I got a jolt that made me bang my head on the underside of the desk. It was the sort of thing that I was happy not to have an audience for.

"Ow. Shit." What the hell had I touched? Under the desk was dark and I could see nothing. I reached in slowly waiting to touch something solid. Nothing, another sweep and a knot of hair was the source. It seemed to be mixed with a herb of some sort. Smelled like sage but I might be wrong. I scooped it into a bag for evidence. Like I give a rat's ass about evidence. I could hear it now.

"M'lord this hair knot gives off supernatural vibes leading me to the accused." Oh yeah, that would be a winner. I can see the old fool in his wig already. Red nose supporting half lens glasses. Too much wine at lunch and a totally befuddled look covering his face.

I still had no clue as to what was going on here. Then it hit me, was the body outside waiting to be killed? Had he put all his affairs in order? I'd check that out later. I would be here in Sunny Gleninch, the land of my youth, investigating the unimaginable. That's me, supernatural sleuth. More like secret squirrel.

Pulling on my coat and closing the door behind me I set off to find a Travel Inn and a bed for a few hours. Then I'd phone in. I couldn't wait, what a great conversation that would be. Priest bludgeoned to death and a vibe from a knot of hair. Joy of joys. The Bishop would be so impressed.

Chapter 2

Travel Inns, motels, call them what you will; they are a modern necessity. I'm in them all the time, a connoisseur you might say. The church like me to be frugal and boy are they frugal. I have to make good use of the congregation's donations. No four star hotels for me. Gleninch has about four different brands of cheap motels. I picked the nearest one. A few raps on the glass doors had brought a sleepy looking night porter to the door. He wasn't impressed with me either. It got better when he got my credit card and realised my holy status. It was 'yes father', 'no father','anything you need father?' On and on. Behaving like a extra from Father Ted.

Amazingly in less than twenty minutes I was back in bed asleep. No longer cold; asleep. The heavy, hollow-fibre, thirty tog duvet wrapped tightly around me. I'd love to say I don't dream but I do. Sometimes in colour, sometimes in glorious technicolour. It all depends what the dream is about; nightmarish images are always colour and childhood memories are always black and white. Odd? Probably. Maybe it's because we had a black and white television when I was young. I never had enough toys either. We were poor in those days. Although in the town of my younger years, everyone was poor but we just didn't know any different. The rows of newly built post war houses were filled with overspills from all over the place and by the time I was born they were full of working class poor folks.

Around nine the constant beep-beep of the phone dragged me from the warm cocoon I had made on the bed. It must have been beeping for some time to rouse me from a deep and dreamless sleep. I pulled myself across the king size bed to put my mobile phone to my ear.

"Steel." I managed to sound mildly grumpy, not pissed off. My face enough to curdle milk. The escaping yawn covered by my hand as I faced away.

"Andrew, did I wake you?" Bishop Michael tried to sound apologetic, his deep voice rumbling. He wanted to know what was going on. Me too. His manners were just so much better than mine and he was obviously a morning person. For him the day was half over by nine o'clock whereas mine rarely ever started before then.

"Yeah. I'll be here a while." I pulled the quilt closely and yawned again quietly away from the phone. I didn't want to let the cool air inside, my bladder would rebel. I hoped that this would be a quick call.

"Oh, I see. Terrible business I hear." His voice sounding like a shocked old lady at a tea dance or high tea. I could almost imaging him fanning himself in shock. I smiled a little at my own humour.

"Beaten to death." I didn't really want to go into it now. I was disinclined to elaborate and the silence began to build. He is a patient man, the Bishop, and he out waited me. He knows me too well.

"I'll mail you a preliminary in a few hours. I don't know what's going on yet. Something is though." I just stopped and waited. So did he, the fly old bugger. It was a return to the cat and mouse we often play.

"Andrew, try and play nicely with the police this time." Bad press was so difficult to explain. A point he never tired of reminding me. Although he never spoke of the event in question, we both knew what he was referring to. I had been recalled for not playing nicely with the police. "They need evidence. Try to get some. I'll call you later." He hung up. No chance for dissent nor reply. Probably just as well, all things considered.

"Okay, bye. Thanks for the wake up call." I spoke to the dead receiver, I was pissed off now. Might as well get on with it, I had received my orders. That's me, non-morning person, filled with the joys of life. At least the room had a shower. And the shower had hot water; oh the sins of the flesh.

It just looks like an ordinary modern church. There is nothing particularly clever about it. White render, mesh over the windows and a close cut well-maintained grassy trim around it. There are probably hundreds of buildings like this all over the central belt of Scotland. Imagination in construction was at a premium at the time, I suppose. This one was an Anglican one. Makes no difference to me which denomination it is. I investigate them all. Funny how ecumenical they can be on this front and bugger all else. Maybe it's because I'm not actually a Priest as such. Well I am, but not really in the traditional way. As I have the gift; I was kind of recruited for this role. Head-hunted as it were, five hundred years ago I'd have been burned at the stake or head-hunted in an entirely different way. Progress. I have been ordained by all the main groups so that I can cause little offence to all sides. I do my best to cause offence as often as possible to anyone who'll listen. Maybe I'll get fired. Yeah right, I wish.

Police tape flapping everywhere. Two police cars and a handful of nosey, bored, spectator-ghouls. I parked behind the yellow luminous stripes of the police car and hoped I would be able to slip in unnoticed. I ducked under the tape and made for the front doors. The polite uniformed bobby intercepted me smoothly and asked what my business was here. His high visibility yellow jacket looked like it had seen better days;

cleaner ones too. He didn't seem to be dialled in to my presence here.

"Where's Brotherton." No attempt at civility on my part as I just want to get inside. The grey weather feels like it will bring rain, just like every other day in Fife at this time of year. I tried not to look too irritated and I don't know if I pulled it off. Not that I care overly much either way.

"Inside. Are you Father Steel? He's expecting you." Deferential and competent, I was beginning to feel less peevish. He managed to ignore my irritation. He had probably had a decent night's sleep though.

"I am. Good morning, Officer. I know the way." I bare my teeth in an attempt to smile at the young man. I'm never really sure how much teeth to show, don't want to look stupid. I just go for something in the middle, enough teeth but not the whole goofy. Smiling should be part of church PR training.

He stepped back and let me pass into the house of God. My domain. The door closed with a solid thud and silence fell heavily in the foyer. I made for the office where I expected to find Brotherton. I was right. Psychic or what?

"Morning." I spoke first and scanned the room. The small office had been searched thoroughly and was a lot less tidy than the last time I was there. You just can't get the staff these days.

"Father Steel. I have been ordered to extend any assistance to you, that you might need." He paused and caught my eye. His hostility was simmering under the surface of those cop eyes. He didn't know why he had to extend anything to the scruffy priest in front of him. Life is full of little mysteries. I serve up my best bland face giving nothing away.

"I don't see why we need help with a fairly straightforward mugging that's lead to murder?" He let it out. He had been holding that one a while. He was not happy at this situation. Orders from on high with no explanation. I wouldn't take kindly to 'do as you are told' as an reason either. I caught his eye and held it for a moment, not challenging just pulling his attention to me.

"I'm not here to walk over your turf Inspector. I'm here to walk on God's turf. Neither of us want to piss Him off now, do we?" I smile, I am so irreverent. The smile reached my eyes, briefly, but at least it got there. I hoped that would break the ice a little.

Brotherton's eyebrow shot up as he tried to decide how serious I was. He had been given orders and would follow them. Good dog. He didn't like the not knowing why, however. There was no sign that my smiled had penetrated his irritation.

"It's not about turf." He managed to squeeze the words out; sullen but not teenager sullen. He was keeping a tight rein on his emotions. He was well trained on that front.

"Whatever, Brotherton. We have to work together to resolve this situation. What have you found out?" That's me, reconciliation personified. The sooner we found out what was going on the sooner I would piss off. It seemed he had grasped that too.

"Not much. The late Father MacPhail was hit on the head and died in his car park. Nothing was stolen. No sign of any attempt to break into the church or the Rectory next door. Nothing suspicious in here." Brotherton paused and glared. He was reporting like a rookie, not an Inspector of twelve years experience. He wasn't happy.

"Go on, you're doing splendidly." I couldn't resist. I am often the oldest child in the room. Sometimes I try not to be but not very often. A deep breath and a bite on his tongue and Brotherton continued.

"We have not entered the Rectory yet; we were waiting for you. I have the keys to the rectory and his car. Not a lot to go on yet. He was well liked, apparently." He concluded his update and waited. Apart from the person who caved his skull in, obviously.

"Inspector, I'm a pain in the ass. I'll try to make this as painless as possible. Let's go take a look. Generally, Priests don't get beaten to death. This is Gleninch, though." My mouth twitched a little, well I tried to look friendly.

"It's the fifth murder this year and it's only February." Brotherton shook his head. He was getting hammered and it was beginning to show. The relentless stream of horrors he would have seen obviously taking its toll.

"How many do you normally get? A year that is?" I asked, five sounded a lot to me. I had grown up here and I remembered a church pianist being beaten to death when I was about ten but no others came to mind. Gleninch wasn't that dangerous or violent.

"Less than five for a year, not five in five weeks." He didn't look very happy, but then again maybe he had been run off his feet. He looked a little ragged at the edges.

"Solved any yet?" It didn't come out right but you know how it is. His face darkened as he turned towards me. Stony would be the right description of his look. I had touched a nerve with my big foot, which was firmly in my mouth.

"We have successful outcomes on each one so far." He was not amused, he probably felt I was questioning his competence. Well I was, in a way. He didn't need to take it personally, though. I was just asking.

"Excellent. Then we'll have this sorted out in no time." The smile I made definitely did not reach my eyes. I led the way, the Rectory was waiting for us, locked up and intact like a virgin waiting to be deflowered. Its secrets to be discovered by the dynamic duo.

We went forth like a couple after a row, all front but with an atmosphere that fooled no one. Mum and Dad had definitely not kissed and made up. The uniformed kids didn't look directly at us as we made our way to the Rectory. The trees, skies, bushes and houses much more interesting than us apparently.

Brotherton handed me the key to the door and I did the honours.

Chapter 3

A little push was all it took to open the door. Welcome mat smiling up at us, 'Jesus Lives..Here'. Interesting choice, I thought. Parquet flooring in a lovely herringbone design leading up the hall just begging to be walked on. A mirror on the wall and coats hanging along side; stairs up on the left. This was so normal looking. Why was it anything but normal? What should have been a sanctuary had my gift tingling my skin and screaming warnings to my brain. We were most definitely in the right place.

I stepped over the threshold and knew then that the problem was mine to solve. I stopped dead in my tracks and Brotherton shunted me forward. I hoped he didn't drive like that. His mumbled apology almost missed as I felt power washing over me. Like a rising tide clambering up my legs and across my torso. The wave of nausea that ran through me was sharp and brought a trickle of bile up my throat, the burning sensation making me cough.

"Sorry Father, I …" He mumbled another apology. I still hadn't moved forward and he was blocked in the doorway. He could tell something wasn't right.

"Brotherton, no one else comes in but us for a while." Orders from the tufty-haired priest. My voice the most grown up one I could muster in the circumstances. I hoped I didn't sound too shaky,

"No problem." He shut the door behind us, and spoke quickly into his radio. The double glazed door closing out the traffic noise with a clunk.

Something flapped over my shoulder, blue latex gloves. Brotherton was interested in the integrity of the evidence, apparently. I pulled them on without too much fumbling and only a few hairs plucked from my wrist. I felt like I was in a cop drama or that forensic one on Satellite television. More like Inspector Clouseau than Inspector Morse. Maybe by the time I had silver hair I'd be good at this although the grey was beginning to make more appearances these days. A silver fox in the making.

I wandered up the hall, every fibre of my being thrumming, some shit was going on here. I did not like the feel of this one little bit. The parquet flooring didn't squeak under our feet, it amplified the sounds of our footfall. MacPhail may have been popular and a pillar of the community but his rectory reeked of supernatural activity. Ahead of me the lounge looked inviting and friendly; a soft sofa and two leather chairs. Books filled a bookcase, and DVD's filled another bookcase. The carpet was an old Axminster style rug, like my granny had owned years ago.

Varnished floorboards surrounded the rug. It all looked so normal and yet I knew it was anything but. The working of magic in this place had been frequent and spanned many years. How had this been kept secret? Surely someone must have suspected at some point? Secrets always find a way out.

Sliding double glazed patio doors led outside to a nice town garden. Sunlight was peeking through a gap in the heavy velour burgundy curtains. I stepped over to them and opened them wide, sunlight had power over the Dark. One fact that the movies never seem to get wrong and it didn't just destroy vampires. It worked on almost anything.

My skin was crawling on its own, trying to get off and run away. A bad case of the hebe-geebees. The room looked like it should, no neon signs pointing to clues. A selection of framed photographs adorned the wall. One or two pictures with Bishops and the like, and one with the First minister of the new Scottish assembly. A right hob-nobber. A few ornaments from Africa on the wall unit among other odds and ends. I walked round the sofa, still tingling. I sat in his seat; the seat of power as it were. It enveloped me as I sank in to its arms.

I felt him then. His presence was filling the room, a malignant, evil, mean and cruel spirit. Priest, Pastor, Minister whatever title suits your flavour best, usually these titles bring a certain expectation of the work of God. Usually, love, faith, charity, compassion that sort of thing can be expected. Father MacPhail was definitely reading from a different scripture. I could feel his essence and he was an utter bastard. This was a room of tears. The emotions in this room were raw and stark and I could feel them. How many had he hurt in here? I felt tears tickling the sides of my face. It happens, I cry. Live with it. Sometimes the tears come unbidden as I feel some of the memories laid down and fed back to me. Experiencing them as if my own. I have long since stopped trying to control them.

"Father, are you all right?" Oh bloody marvellous. Brotherton chose now to look in. He looked a bit confused, it might have been embarrassment. How often do grown men cry for no good reason? I do it all the time.

"I'm just peachy." I do nothing about the tears. I act like they are not there, it works for me. Most people just play along and ignore them too. The 'Don't stare' training we give children always seems to kick in.

"There will be some evidence here. I'll find it." I stated. Brotherton looked a bit bemused. He had no idea what my way of working might be nor why I was the empowered pain in the ass. He seemed to accept my statement at face value though.

"I've looked upstairs and the kitchen and all is neat and orderly. I don't think the killer was in here." His words sounded a little too matter-of-fact for my liking. Of course the killer wasn't in here, that's not really in question. Never argue with a psychic, I always want to say. It always comes out differently though.

"Brotherton, I'll check out the upstairs. I don't like this at all." I was so glad to get out of that seat. Just like that MacPhail left me, thank God. What a bastard he had been. He had enjoyed inflicting the pain both mental and physical.

Three rooms upstairs and a bathroom. Over specified for a single man, if you ask me. I start in his bedroom. I dislike the décor immediately, jealous of the high standards that MacPhail lived in. The dado rail splitting the vertical striped paper from the,tonally matching, painted upper section. The pile on the carpet was deep and soft, and new. No doubt it felt lovely between the toes. I didn't think the colour matched the wallpaper.

"You can't hide from me you bastard." I state flatly to the room. I could feel the carnality like a breeze in my face. A parade of partners had warmed the bed. Both genders and a mixture of ages I was sure. I know corruption when it kisses my skin. Brotherton would need evidence. Fuck that. I remove the latex glove and lean forward. My hand lightly touched the sheet, Egyptian cotton no doubt.

A mixed patina of essences flew through me and I get a totally unwanted view of the most recent bed warmers. This bed is a busy place; there had been a few recently. I screw my eyes shut and get a picture of MacPhail and his depravity. A slim form face down, followed quickly by a rather fat older woman on her knees. I open my eyes quickly to dispel the image. Not an image I want to keep. Vivid and strong it had been burned into me and was so difficult to unsee. I need brain bleach to get that out but it will be stuck there for all time, it's just the way my memory works. Total flash recall and never what I want to remember.

I can't miss the mixture of lust, pain and cruelty that fills the bedroom. I can feel that this is no ordinary rectory. I've seen, and felt, some hairy stuff but this is right up there. A mixture of sex, pain and supernatural power fill the whole bloody place. Like a cocktail of all things debauched and dangerous. I open the bedside drawer and find nothing. It is empty, nothing. My bedside cabinet is full of letters, junk and all sorts of oddments. MacPhail has an empty drawer. The tidiest priest I've ever seen. What the hell was he doing? Tidying up before I got here? Or did someone else do it? Shit. I am a bit slow, sometimes.

"Brotherton." I call, without barking. Although there might have been a growl buried in there somewhere. I hope I don't need to shout again because invariably that is a bark. I hear him on the stairs and I start speaking before he gets into the bedroom.

"Who called this in? Everything has been tidied up or removed." I state quickly. He flipped out his notebook and flipped through the pencil scrawls until a name jumped out.

"Anonymous caller I'm afraid." Brotherton shook his head. He wasn't even surprised, just disappointed. Modern times and no one wanting to get involved. This time I think the caller was involved.

"Surprising isn't it?" I can be a little sarcastic on occasion. This was one of those. I had that near sneer on my lips that is one of my best looks.

"Not really. Most 999 calls are anonymous. People don't want to get involved." Brotherton explained. At least he looked apologetic. It was something.

"Who can blame them eh?" I try not to look too sour but not really pulling it off. I do understand there is nothing to be done about it now.

"Doesn't explain the tidy up job, though. Why would the rectory need tidied up? What needed to be hidden?" Brotherton frowned. It seemed to me that he didn't like it either. His blue eyes looked cold and serious, first time I noticed anything about him. We might need to get along for a while. I am not good at getting along, apparently.

"Well we'd better go through the motions." I smile to myself. I always liked the double entendre. Okay, I know it's a disgusting idea but whatever gets me through the day.

In all the rooms there are essences and vibrations that make me feel pretty woozy and I feel almost a little tipsy. Even the bathroom. I mean the bathroom for fucks sake, what supernatural shit takes place in the bathroom. Well I had to find that out. There was a strange looking bar above the shower, I decided that I knew what it was for. There was no way I was touching it. After having touched his sheets I didn't want to watch his pornographic life any further. I decided to check out the sink.

I made a bit of a mess. I became a plumber for the morning and hauled off the sink trap expecting evidence and clues to be contained in the gooey sludge that lived there. Brotherton wasn't entirely happy at the mess I made of the floor but he was impressed that I thought of it. The sludge was bagged and tagged. I couldn't reach under the bath panel so I left it alone. The trap under the bath could wait.

His home office was a bit more like it. It wasn't totally tidied up. The beige computer sitting proudly on the desk was begging me to touch its keyboard. It was probably a good idea to leave that to the specialists. The last time I had tried to interrogate a computer on a case I had set us back months in terms of evidence. I moved the mouse with the back of my hand and the screen leapt to life. A lovely view of the countryside and the dreaded password request. Bloody typical. It already had a sticker on the top, asking for it to be taken for analysis. Brotherton had been through this room.

"I have an address book from the desk." He chimed from the doorway, seeing me scanning the desk. I didn't turn round, I just let my eyes rove across the surface waiting for inspiration to strike.

"That will be useful." I meant it but probably sounded a bit sarcastic. I would be looking through it later hoping that someone or something jumped out at me. I pulled the top drawer out of the desk and looked inside. If it was anything like my desk, things fell down inside at the back. I couldn't really see so I reached inside. I felt something and pulled it out. Like little Jack Horner I had pulled out a plum. It was an envelope with Polaroids in it.

"Ah ha." I couldn't resist. Of course I had left fibres from my sleeve all over the edge, hopefully no one would notice this minor contamination but I had put my gloves back on earlier so no prints. I waved the envelope in the air. Brotherton was over in a flash. We looked at the photos together, all six of them. If I wasn't so sex deprived I would have been upset but I was simply envious. MacPhail, I presume, was the male in the photos and there were three different women in them. Not a face in sight, though, but it might be fun trying to identify them.

"I wonder who these ladies might be?" I mused, aloud. I think I sounded a bit of a sanctimonious prigg but too bad. I couldn't keep a little smirk from twitching my lips.

"Members of the congregation?" Brotherton was catching

on. We might sort this mess out after all. We both knew there was much more than the beating to death about this case.

"Probably. Not the usual activities of pastoral care. MacPhail was busy." I smirked wider this time, I just couldn't help it. The inner juvenile escaped in time to dispel my grown up success of finding evidence.

"I'll have forensics tear this place apart and that computer. We'll have a better idea once we have done that. Maybe a jealous husband or lover?" He was getting all efficient on me just like a proper detective. I didn't feel the need to say that neither of those were likely.

"Let's go. I need to report in." Things were going to be very interesting.

We were standing together at the foot of the stairs about to leave. Brotherton had locked the back door and had radioed the forensic crew to proceed. I looked up and saw it. A loft hatch. Upstairs hall and a loft hatch. All these houses had them. I looked at Brotherton and flicked my eyes upstairs. Did I need to spell it out? Apparently, I did.

"What?" He was confused by my clue. Maybe it was the untidy eyebrows that did it. Perhaps I had over estimated how efficient he was as a detective. Maybe both.

"There is a loft up there. I want to look." Direct I think it is called. Abrasive, it certainly is.

"Hold off on that crew." He sighed into his radio microphone. He was following his orders to the letter, extend all aid as required. The little sunshine had stopped peeking out from his cloud and he was back to grey and brooding. He obviously felt that I was going to be a burden that he alone would have to bear. Just like Eeyore.

"After you." I gesture up the stairs.

Moments later we have found the rod used to open the loft and pull down the stainless steel ladder. B&Q's finest loft ladder kit installed by a professional not some botch of a DIY job. Brotherton produces a large torch and turns it on. Where he had it I do not know but I want to call him Pockets. Probably not the best idea as we are still in the getting to know you phase, only our second date as it were. It is time to ascend into the inner sanctum. Now we were making progress, the loft would tell us all we needed, I hoped. I was betting that MacPhail hid all his shit in the loft. I know I did as a kid.

Chapter 4

Lofts are amazing places. When I was young I spent ages in our loft. It was floored and carpeted. It was a cool den, of course, it was bloody cold in the winter. My friends and I used to hang out up in the loft and read girlie magazines and lie about our prowess with the ladies. Those were the days, gone and never to return. I doubted MacPhail had any girlie magazines up here. His was into a more hands on kind of lifestyle.

It came as no surprise to me that Macphail's loft wasn't cold. It was lined with board and carpeted and had an interesting skylight window in the roof. No, it was positively luxurious. No spiders, nor webs for that matter, to make me cringe. It did, however, have a telescope and lots of star charts. Apart from being an utter bastard, who obviously got my ration of sex, he was an astronomer. Stargazer of a serious vent, if the telescope was anything to go by, it looked very pricey. Not a forty nine pounds starter from Argos but a great big round one with all sorts of attachments. Cost was no object, apparently, when it came to his toys. This was a toy with a purpose and I was betting I wouldn't like what he did with it. Brotherton whistled under his breath, he was impressed too. Like some things, size matters.

"Good call, Father." He was warming up to me. Everyone does, eventually. Yeah right. We stood looking, not really wanting to touch anything, until we both set off at once our fingers reaching for clues.

"I had a train set in my loft. He obviously kept his toy in the loft, too." I didn't want to be too smug. I think I got the balance just right. Two in a row and all that. The smirk that played around the edge of my mouth wasn't juvenile in the least.

"There is some very expensive stuff here." Brotherton was on the money. A statement of the obvious is a good way to start. He was scanning the room looking for obvious clues, poor soul. I doubt any of the clues here would be of the obvious variety. Police training is probably not big on occult or astronomy.

"Let's see what he was looking at." What I know about astronomy you can write neatly on the rear of a postage stamp, and not one of the big ones either. I can bluff with the best though. I look at the telescope and see a power cord, which I switch on before I put my eye to the eyepiece. Luckily for the amateur that I am, it is not pointed at the sun. Or it would have been curtains for my eyeball, it would have been fried. It's daytime so I have proven my lack of knowledge, better to do this after dark. I will come back later. I move away from the all-seeing eye. It sits on some sort of motorised thing. Well I dunno what it is called, like a track that it would move on. Looks complicated.

"Does it matter what he's looking at? As long as it's not someone's bedroom window?" Brotherton was looking round, inspiration failing to strike. The training at Tulliallan Police College is very much an inside the box style of thing.

I opened the drawer of his immaculate desk, it even felt expensive. Usually priests are recipients of hand me downs but MacPhail appeared to be well to do. Nothing in the whole house contradicted this. Smoothly it slid open, inside some star charts with lines on them. I hoped these were what we, in the business, call clues. I picked them up.

"Inspector, I'll need these examined." I spoke with certainty I didn't feel. I tried to look like I knew what they might mean.

"Examined for what? Fingerprints?" Poor man really had no idea. His face was showing that very fact. I was pleased that he indulged my search of the house, after all the body had been found outside.

"I was thinking more by an astronomer. What do these lines mean?" I waved them about a bit.

"Will it be related to the murder?" His scepticism was really unbecoming. After all I had found the photos. To say I was a little disappointed by his lack of seeing the wider picture would be an understatement.

"Probably not, but it will help me find out what's actually going on." I could have explained but I didn't. He just had to do as I asked him.

"I'll see what I can do." The ubiquitous plastic evidence bag appeared in his hand waiting for my deposit of the clue. I am sure they are just freezer bags with printing on them. I duly dropped them inside, knowing that they were probably meaningless.

"I am sure I know someone at the museum if you need help." I was trying to be helpful, I hoped he realised that. I don't always offer up my experts. Sharing my toys was one thing I never learned at nursery school.

"Shall I let the SOCO boys in?" I nodded. It was unlikely that I would get my hat-trick of clues. This house was giving me a headache anyway. Way too much monkey mojo for this time in the day. Besides my grumbling stomach was telling me that breakfast was the most important meal of the day. Pity I had missed it. Well it was seven pounds fifty. Bloody rip off, if you ask me.

"Bishop Michael please." I managed to be polite, just. The gatekeeper didn't sound all that friendly nor deferential.

"Can I put you on hold?" No time to say no as the music began, Gregorian chanting. For goodness sake how bloody predictable. Never mind I was almost humming along when it stopped to be replaced by my boss.

"Andrew, how are things going?" He was way too cheerful, disgustingly, cheerful. The absolute opposite to how I felt after the visit to the manse.

"Well Bishop, I have searched his house and it stinks of activity. Sex and depravity all over it." Why was I so coy about saying supernatural? I always feel embarrassed as I say it, so I avoid it. It just sounds idiotic.

"That is not good. I need you to wrap this up quickly if you can. I have something else for you to deal with soon. Are you getting help from the local police?" He asked. What he really meant was 'are you playing nicely?'

"They have been very good. Inspector Brotherton has extended every courtesy. They are looking into MacPhail's computer and some star charts. He was an astronomer as well as a dabbler in something." I swigged from my coffee cup and it was cold. Cold coffee is an acquired taste, one I have never acquired. I almost spat as my tongue recoiled.

"Send the charts on to me and I'll get them examined by our people for any religious significance. Oh and Andrew, keep the news of his behaviours out of the press if you can." It would be a PR disaster if word got out about a shagging priest and his flock. Maybe years ago but not these days, it was almost expected. Besides, didn't shepherds have previous with their sheep?

"I'll try Bishop. Do you want Brotherton to destroy the Polaroids?" I knew I was pushing my luck, especially after the evidence reminder.

"I don't think that will be necessary. Just don't want them appearing in the Sunday papers. Or any other paper for that matter." He was getting bored. I can tell when I bore people. It is like another side to my gift. Let me be anything but a bore.

"OK will do my very best. I'll call tomorrow." Sarcasm was beginning to creep in. Best not to antagonise the Bishop, after all, he sends me out to play.

"All right Andrew. Good luck and you be careful." The phone call was over. I had reported in. I also had not made it sound like I was totally clueless. One back for me.

What the hell was I going to do now? I couldn't exactly go round the congregation asking who was sleeping with MacPhail. I should probably start with the members of the Vestry, the committee that run the church at a local level. I'd get the names from Brotherton.

"Inspector Brotherton? Steel here. Can you give me the names of the members of the Vestry at St Margaret's?" Straight in at the jugular, no messing with small talk. I find the less I say the less chance that I'll piss someone off.

"Yes I have a pen. OK, go ahead." And just like that I had a list of possibles. One of them at least knew what was going on.

Time to put on my Spanish inquisition robes and go biting the guilty. Well more a subterfuge over the tragedy. The lamp in the eyes could wait till later. I wondered if Brotherton had a lamp all set up. He didn't strike me as the type.

Chapter 5

There is a reason that I am not a regular Priest. Well actually there are loads but the main one is that I am a lousy conversationalist. It's true. I really can't feign that much interest and after the pleasantries are exchanged then that's where the difficulty starts. I ask you, what do I have to say to an eighty year old woman who thinks the world is a den of iniquity? She has a point, of course, but it gets a bit wearing. Then there's the apologising for every bloody or damn that passes their lips, like I am fragile and will faint at a little swear word. Pisses me off. However, the main issue I have is the tea. Cups and cups of tea. Plates of biscuits brought out especially for the visit of the priest. Small wonder so many of my brothers are portly.

"It's terrible these days. Who would do such a thing to a man of god? It's just terrible." She was obviously in shock. It was a bad world out there, one which she obviously didn't understand. Her scrunched up hankie dabbed at her nose, a sniff as vocal accompaniment. What the hell was I going to say now? I am really crap at the pastoral empathy bit. Maybe while she was a bit unsettled I could pump her for information. What a callous bastard I am. There was no hint of anything in my area in this house. I waited for a hundred. A slow hundred before I opened my big mouth.

"Well Mrs McLaughlin, you must have seen a few Rectors in your time here?" I thought I might as well let her ramble on a bit, who knows what might turn up. She was, after all, the longest serving member of the vestry committee. If there were any skeletons buried in the congregation, she would know where, when and who. Probably even the why.

"Oh well, Father Andrew, that's true. I have been a member of St Margaret's since it was built for the new town in the early fifties." She smiled proudly. A long association made her one of the Holy.

"You've seen many changes then?" Just priming the pump, as it were. Or avoiding putting my foot in it too quickly. I smiled gently to the old dear, encouraging her to recount the stories of the past.

"Oh yes. From such a small congregation we've grown until there are more than four hundred on the roll and more than two hundred on a Sunday." Stats like a football commentator, next she'll be telling me what they've won. We did the double in 1995, perhaps a treble and a European cup too. She was off and running. The achievements were remarkable, if you like that sort of thing.

"That's a big crowd for a Sunday, how do you manage it?" I sounded suitably in awe. After all attendances had been dropping, at worship, like a stone and this one bucked the trend.

"Father MacPhail, Lord bless his soul," she paused to cross herself and take a breath to avoid more tears, "was very popular among the younger members of the congregation." I almost choke on my digestive crumbs. Was she telling me something?

"Scripture union? Youth fellowship? That sort of thing?" Just giving her some rope to hang herself with. The rope I hoped would tie up a few loose ends about MacPhail.

"Well those too. He was a very handsome man after all." So much left unsaid. Just a big enough hint for me. I don't think she meant it though. It might just have been me projecting a meaning into her words.

"It always helps attract new people to the church. His sermons must have been very modern too I suppose." Hopefully she didn't approve. Some parishioners dislike change with a passion.

"Well I suppose so, but he always remembered the more traditional messages too. He was good for the parish." A maudlin look began to settle on her face. She obviously liked the man. I wonder how much she knew. Probably nothing but I'd bet she could guess plenty. The faraway look passed to one with tears at the edges, her front was cracking.

"I'm sure he was." I'd decided to let her get her equilibrium back a little before I asked her for the minutes of the meetings. A moment passed.

"The Bishop sent me over as soon as the news broke this morning. I will be with you until something more permanent can be arranged." I shifted slightly in my seat as I got ready to make my request. If you ever play poker against me, I am in trouble. I have too many tells apparently. The old dear barely noticed. She nodded her understanding.

"'Be tactful Andrew, it is a time of great shock' he told me, and of course I understand how many of you must feel." I paused, all sincerity and sympathy, "So that I can get up to speed with Father MacPhail's duties I need to look over the vestry minutes. It will be so much simpler than bothering the members at this sad time." I smiled softly all full of concern that I didn't feel. I needed a flaming clue as to what was happening and had to start somewhere.

"Of course, I have copies. Let me get them for you." She painfully hoisted herself from her chair and ambled from the room. No doubt she had a folder going all the way back to the fifties.

The second she closed the door behind herself I stood up and looked at the pictures inside the dresser cabinet over by the window. Inside the frames were a variety of pictures, some obviously family, others with Father MacPhail and assorted others. I have a good memory for faces and stared hard at the group photos, hoping that later I might see some of these people again. Names are a little more difficult. I had just re-parked my backside beside the biscuits when she came in with a handful of typed minutes for me.

"These are the minutes of the last three Vestry meetings Father." She handed them to me without any further explanation. She was obviously distracted. Why the last three meetings I wonder? Who knows but maybe I was over thinking it. A few more minutes of banality and I was on my way through the door offering platitudes of consolation and sympathy.

Interesting reading they were not. Dull, dull, dull. The minutiae of the details of these vestry meetings was telling me bugger all. Finances look fine. Points made at the meeting bore little resemblance to anything sinister. Total waste of time, the lot of it. The good people who participate in the running of churches give a lot of their time to make it work. Why did it have to be so very boring? Probably because they were generally older men and women who longed for control of something. It was a sad place to try and gain fulfilment. I was a little grateful that Mrs MacLaughlin had only given me three doses of this drivel to read. After all she could have given me years worth. I had just decided to go to the police station and see Brotherton when the phone rang. Not my mobile phone, but the room phone. I hadn't given the number to anyone except Brotherton or the Bishop.

"Yes." Neutrality achieved. No clues that this was a surprise.

"Stay away. Or you'll regret it." A voice heavy with malice rolled down the line towards me. Sounded like one too many old gangster movies had influenced the caller. I was betting he wasn't a really bad man. Just a wannabe.

"Piss off." Didn't expect that, did he. A click and the conversation was over. I smiled. It usually took me a couple of days to alienate the locals, I had managed it in less than an afternoon. I laughed to myself. Progress. The phone rang again

"What?" I snapped. I was just pretending though. I hoped he was calling back for round two, after all I had knocked him off his stride.

"Father Steel? Brotherton here." He sounded confused. Doesn't everyone snap down the phone?

"Sorry I thought you were someone else." I was smirking like an idiot now. Poor Brotherton having to work with me.

"Preliminary post mortem report is in. Do you want to come down to the station? I am at Rowan Road local station. Do you know where it is?" He was trying to be helpful, bless him. I grew up in this town and knew where it was.

"I'll be there in ten minutes. I know where it is." It was less than four hundred yards from where I grew up. I could find it in a blackout.

"I'll put the kettle on." Brotherton was extending an olive branch. He must want to know something. Well he'd better be patient because I am not the sharing kind. I pulled on my coat, it was raining again. Actually it hadn't really stopped. Yep that's what I remembered about Gleninch, pissing rain and grey skies. Oh yeah and a bloody cold wind off the North Sea. Why do the natives stay? I had no idea.

Chapter 6

Fan belt screaming like a banshee, it was better than a siren. I couldn't really see much through the misted windscreen but that was just too bad. I could find the Rowan Road station in the dark with a blindfold. I used to lust after a girl called Helen who lived just around the corner from it. I smiled as I remembered her. A priest should not be having these impure thoughts I chastised myself. Well actually, I just enjoyed the reverie. She was pretty, after all. We had a great time for a while, amazing how much fun you can have at fifteen.

The houses had changed very little, the trees a little bigger, and the cars in the streets more modern. Overall Gleninch was like the Eternal City, unchanging. It was still a dormitory not really sure what to be. The new town experiments after the war were not really the success that was hoped for. Overspill populations from the west coast transplanted to the east coast. A recipe for success, I don't think.

Rowan Road Police Station, was the headquarters in Gleninch for years, but had since been replaced by a newer building further from the town centre. It was a masterpiece of utilitarian design, dull and functional in the extreme. I had been here a few times before. The first time, I was eight, on a school trip. I had freaked out in the cells after the kind policeman had locked me in, 'to let me see what it was like'. An early form of aversion therapy I presume. Unfortunately I could feel all the ills that the many inhabitants of that cell had perpetrated on their victims. It gave me nightmares for weeks. Not a nice experience for an eight year old psychic sensitive.

I drove into the rear car park beside all the luminescent yellow chequered traffic cars, enjoying my exalted status. I was hoping to meet unibrow boy, but that was wishful thinking on my part. I got out, pressed my remote locking as I turned away and began to march towards the service entrance. I had my dog collar on, in uniform, I looked the part apart from the stubborn sticking up tuft at the back.

Brotherton met me at the back door. He was looking a bit too friendly for my liking. He had a smile on his face, all white teeth. I bared mine back at him as best I could and he ushered me inside. He marched past the various offices until we came to an interview room. He sat facing the door and I had the perp's seat. The report was in a manilla file. All official looking. Brotherton slid it across the desk to me. I opened the report and read it. The silent waiting doesn't bother me but I expect Brotherton uses it regularly.

I have no real idea what half the words actually meant but the best I could do was work out that blunt force trauma was what killed him. I didn't need the report to tell me that. I had seen the dent in his cranium. I took a while to flick through the rest, I said nothing. I just waited and then after, what I hoped was long enough, put it down on the desk. I looked at Brotherton.

"What do you think Father?" He asked me, like I should know. He seemed a little too smug for my liking but I was still waiting for his great reveal.

"What? Skull stove in? A mystery isn't it." It was a little too sarcastic. Never mind eh? Must try harder next time.

"The Toxicology report, I meant." He was unflappable. Bloody detectives. He was dragging this out and I was not really sure where he was going.

"Oh sorry, I never looked at that bit." I looked a little sheepish, I had been found out.

"He had a hell of a cocktail in his blood. I am amazed he could stand." Brotherton opened the report and handed me the toxicologist report. More chemical stuff, I had no idea.

"Tell me what I'm reading Inspector. I don't know what half this stuff is?" No point in bluffing and bullshitting. He would need to spell it out for me. My degree was most certainly not pharmacology.

"Ketamine. They use that to sedate horses. It also has

hallucinogenic effects. On the streets it's called Vitamin K. Heavy stuff." Brotherton looked at me. All was clear now then, apparently.

"So he took drugs?" I am a bit slow sometimes, maybe if he had given me coffee and biscuits I might have been better placed to keep up.

"The amount of Ketamine in his blood, he probably couldn't stand let alone walk. Pathologist thinks he might have even been in a coma before the blow to the head killed him. Might even have been from his head hitting the pavement." Brotherton, looked a little bit happy. Now I knew why. If it wasn't murder then I would be out of his hair.

"Could the Ketamine have been administered later?" All CSI now, like a pro. I knew he had been murdered, no doubt about it. I also knew that there was something hinky going on, regardless of his report.

"Doc says no chance, well and truly through his system. It was inhaled." Brotherton was hanging on to misadventure like a terrier to a rat. After all, the most obvious reason is usually the right one. Brotherton seemed keen to not look too far past the end of his nose.

"Brotherton, he was murdered. End of." I was getting a bit bored with this and my shirtyness seemed to be on the increase.

"'There's evidence to suggest he may have fallen over,

banged his head in a drug induced haze and died where he fell. On K you feel next to nothing that happens to your body." He was being patient with the new boy.

"Did we find an inhaler? Any Ketamine in the house? Better have a look then." I moved on as he shook his head. To leap to assumptions about what killed MacPhail was just sloppy police work. Brotherton didn't strike me as the kind who was sloppy. Maybe he was, who knows. The happy demeanour had evaporated like stink off a turd. He shut the file and stood up, looked like we were going back to the scene. I noticed the absence of the cup of tea and Rich Tea biscuit. Probably best not to mention it. Don't really like Tea that much anyway.

We would be going in his car. Suited me fine. I wondered if he would crack first and start up a conversation. I gave him a minute tops, once we were in the car. I was right.

"Just what are you doing here Father?" Curiosity had got him at last. He had to know.

"I am here because the Home Office called me the other night." I was being bland and obtuse. Skills I have in spades. I was going to make him work for an explanation. Well he started it with the Ketamine stuff.

"Why was I ordered to give you anything you need?" Brotherton's hands were griping the steering wheel quite tightly. I noticed the tension filling his voice and his large frame.

"Good manners maybe?" I laughed gently and then went on, "I deal with crimes against religion. It's my area." Everything and nothing.

"This isn't hate crime. This is a simple death by misadventure or a murder. What do you need to be involved for?" He wasn't happy at my evasions. Life is so hard.

"Brotherton, all crimes against the Church are checked by me and if I deem it necessary to stay for a while, I do. If I think that the local police can manage I let them. It is really that simple."

His brows lowered a bit further. He was not happy. Luckily we were almost there. The psychic realm of terror that was the home of the dead body we had on ice. Ketamine my arse. We would find nothing supporting drug use and I knew it. A little smile was failing to stay off my face.

Chapter 7

"No sign of any drug equipment." Brotherton's faith in misadventure was wavering. I smiled to myself. I am usually right. It's a trait that gets on everyone's nerves eventually. Sometimes that eventually can be measured in minutes.

"I'm not saying he didn't take it, but he was murdered." I tried not to be too smug. Another failure in my many flawed character.

"Why would he take it? He's a pillar of the community? Responsible and well respected." Brotherton was thinking aloud.

"He was also a sexual predator who would sleep with anything that moved." Oops did I just let that out. Yep I did and I meant to. Now whatdya think Inspector?

"What?" Brotherton had a stunned look on his face. He hadn't expected that series of words to fill the air between us.

"Sit down Brotherton and I'll tell you why I am here." He sat on the couch. I wasn't sitting down in here again.

"What I am telling you is covered by the official secrets act 1989 and following and failure to observe the tenets of that act can lead to prosecution." I paused, I like doing this bit. I have had a bit of practice. "Of course you'd lose your job, pension and employment prospects if you decide to ignore my warning." I went on. He nodded, good boy.

"I am an instrument of the Church and the Home office. I am psychically gifted and can feel things." No emotion on my face. He knew I wasn't pissing about.

"Really? But how?" He was a bit babbly but otherwise he believed me. His acceptance was a promising start.

"If the supernatural is involved then it's my area. MacPhail, as it turns out, was a bad man involved in something even worse. I am not sure yet what it is." I paused to let him catch up. He was silent, obviously thinking.

"Are you a religious man Inspector?" I looked straight at him and waited. He shook his head a little. He obviously didn't want to say no.

"Not really. Not been to church in years. It's the job." He seemed apologetic. I am not surprised though, five murders in as many weeks would be awfully hard to reconcile with a good god.

"Find some faith. You'll need it." I smiled. I knew he was one of the good guys. Only problem was that he could see evil all around and could never see any evidence of God. Admittedly I have to look hard to find him too, sometimes. I knew Brotherton was going to be vital to me if I was to work out what was going on. So we needed to be on the same page.

"Why would he take Ketamine then?" He asked, his voice just not getting it. The small things, it seemed, bugged him too.

"Did you not say it had hallucinogenic qualities? Maybe he was looking to see the spiritual world? Or maybe he was given it when unconscious and on the ground?" I thought the first more likely than the idea of post-mortem addition. Now I was thinking out loud. Wasn't really helping.

"What are we missing here? Something is going on behind the façade of normality and we need to work it out." I was pacing around the room. One thing was for sure there was more than MacPhail in on it. I scratched my head, making the tuft at the back stick up. I was managing to keep the room's mojo out but it was tiring.

"What do we actually know?" Brotherton spoke quietly. Back to basics seemed a reasonable place to start. Of course, sometimes it can be a very short list.

"MacPhail is dead. Murdered by someone or something." I began as I paced about. Sherlock Holmes time. I stared out the patio doors looking into the well manicured garden. He must have had a gardener; it was so well kept and tidy. He certainly would not have had any energy left over for gardening.

"We also know someone tidied up after the event." Brotherton added from the couch. He was right but how he could sit there and feel nothing was beyond me.

"I don't like knowing the square root of fuck all." I growled to the room. I saw Brotherton's eyebrows shoot up. He obviously had not heard a priest swear before. He caught his face quickly and looked away.

"Let's get SOCO to pull this place apart." That's the spirit. I smiled to Brotherton and nodded. Let's just turn the place over and see what was under every stone. Let us shine the light into the dark corners and see what scurries out.

"Great idea. Can we keep it quiet? I have had a warning call already." I told him, now we were best buddies and all.

"You should have told me." Brotherton gave me the cop look filled with disappointment at my lack of full disclosure. I shrugged.

"I just did." There we go, obtuse as ever. Brotherton just shook his head as he called in the crime scene forensics team.

Bloody amazing what technology can turn up. I might get an impression here and there but hi tech gizmos are truly amazing. Who would have seen the outline of a pentagram drawn in blood on the polished wooden floor? With an ultra violet light all became apparent. MacPhail was indeed a follower of the Dark. No wonder the living room made me feel queasy. Of course we were really no further forward. I already knew he was bad to the bone. The revelation of the pentagram made little real difference. What he had done with it was something else. A blood pentagram suggests a real practitioner not merely a dilettante.

So now I knew that this was some serious shit. Shock and horror. No idea what flavour of course. That would come later.

Chapter 8

When I decided to visit all the members of the vestry committee I thought it was a good idea. However, after three visits and no progress, I was beginning to change my mind. I had sat on three very uncomfortable couches and tasted a variety of teas. I had learned nothing. It was like a normal congregation so far; an annoyingly bland congregation that loved its priest. All good except the priest in question was a Satanist and all round bad guy.

I was getting a bit pissy, as I usually do when things are not going to plan. Which probably makes me pissy most of the time. However, my luck was about to change. It's funny how these things happen. I don't usually get much of an impression off of people when they are alive but when I shook hands with Angela Brookes, wife of David Brookes the treasurer, I got a surprise. She was a rather attractive thirty something. Not that being attractive was unusual. It was the image I received from her. She was one of the last bed partners of MacPhail. I could see her fucking the living daylights out of him like a lioness in heat. It was all I could do to be coherent. She didn't notice.

"Come in Father, my husband isn't home." Did I catch just a hint of a possibility? I hoped not. I know that I am not irresistible to women. I might like to be, just once, but the reality is that I am so very average in looks and a bit too slim to be all that manly. Her smile was full of potential, or at least I thought so.

"Will he be long?" Great line eh? Spent hours working that one out, the delivery was lame too.

"Unfortunately not Father." I hadn't been imagining her willingness after all. "Would you like some tea?" she seemed disappointed.

"Thank you." She led the way into the, rather sterile, modern furnished living room. She obviously had a lot of spare time on her hands. The laminate flooring was cleaned and held a lovely polish. There was little to identify who might live here. A couple of photos stood upon the mantelpiece. One was a loving family portrait, Angela, David and a lovely younger female version of them. She looked about fourteen. It was a picture like millions of others on mantelpieces the world over. The other was a church outing of some sort.

"Milk and sugar Father?" Her voice came from the kitchen as the kettle began to boil. I couldn't care less actually, with or without, it was probably tasteless. "Both please." I walked over to look out the window. This could be an opportunity. Not to get laid but to get some serious information. If she thought I was one of MacPhail's ilk she might just let something, other than her virtue, slip. I hoped so.

"There we are." She smiled sweetly as she placed the tray on the table. A plate of biscuits accompanied the tea. Nothing too fancy just digestives and hobnobs.

She sat down demurely lifting her tea, a picture of the women's institute if ever there was one. Skirt at the knee and a pressed blouse with two buttons undone. Not a hint of what she hid beneath. From where I was sitting, she looked in very fine shape.

"Terrible business." I shook my head ruefully, imply everything say nothing.

"Oh yes, poor Father MacPhail. He will be sorely missed." Funny how there was little sadness in her voice. I wonder what she would be missing. I kept the smirk contained and sipped once more. It was tasteless.

"I will be helping run things for a while." Okay it was a little fib, but it backed up my hunch. It was true to a degree. After all the Bishop had sent me to deal with the interregnum.

"I am glad. What happened? To Father MacPhail, I mean." She wanted all the gory details that I could share that with her. I could feel her interest rising.

"He was beaten to death outside his home, in the car park. A random mugging apparently." I made it sound so ordinary. So unremarkable. So new town.

"Oh how terrible." She paused, a little catch in her breath " Was it bad?" She was a blood thirsty one.

"Very bloody. Repeated blows to his head and face." I lied smoothly, who would ever find out. I was just playing to my audience. I could tell what she wanted to hear and what would help me find out more.

"Oh my goodness that is awful." It was almost erotic to her. Her eyes sparkled and her lips parted just a little. A flush beginning on her neck and her cheeks pinking a little.

"Yes it is. Who do I need to meet in the congregation, to let me find my feet as it were?" It was suitably vague and might just do the trick. If she was sleeping with MacPhail she was in on it. Her eyes sharpened a little before she answered.

"Let your eyes guide you in your search." Fuck, it was a password. I looked back as I sipped my tea. That was it buggered. My plan hanging in tatters.

"Mom!" A shout from the front door as their daughter arrived. She had saved my bacon, I hoped. The living room door opened and a rather pretty young lady in a school uniform burst in. A tornado all on her own.

"Mom, can I go to a sleepover at Hannah's tonight, please?" She wasn't really asking. She was all grown up in all the wrong places. If she was fifteen I would have been surprised. If she were my daughter, I might just have been locking her in a tower. I doubted the local boys were safe with her around; their little hearts broken repeatedly I expect.

"Your father will be home soon, you can ask him." Angela smiled sweetly. I wondered what she really thought. A huff of displeasure exploded from the daughter.

"Michelle, this is Father Andrew. He will be at St Margaret's for a while." The look that I received was a very strange response to a simple statement. She looked a little wary of me. Not what I expected at all. Was MacPhail a predator on the youngsters too? I kept a straight face nonetheless.

"Pleased to meet you, Michelle." It was as neutral as I could make it and not give myself away. I hoped I was wrong. I could feel the anger inside begin to burn at me like acid reflux. MacPhail was lucky to be already dead or I might have helped him along that road.

"Nice to meet you, too, Father." She smiled, it had a speculative quality about it. She must have learned it from her mother. God help her father, and anyone she used that smile on.

"Wait until your father comes in and ask him. I have no objections to you staying overnight.' Angela sounded so reasonable. So very Mother's Union.

"Speak of the Devil." The front door opened and in walked

the head of the household, a weedy little man, who seemed as down trodden as Horace wimp. I could see immediately who wore the trousers in this house. He was at least third in the pecking order.

"Hi Honey, I'm home." A greeting spouted forth in many a household. He walked in to the living room to be immediately harassed for permission. Which he duly gave. Resistance was futile.

"Darling this is Father Steel. He will be at Saint Margaret's, after what happened to Father MacPhail." As if that said everything; well it did, kind of. He finished hanging up his jacket and crossed towards me.

"Good to meet you Father." He took my hand, he was a little limp. I looked into his eyes as I returned greetings.

"I wanted to chat to you about the vestry, trying to catch up and cause as little disruption as possible." I smiled. I was getting very slick at this particular set of untruths. Practice making perfect.

"Of course. Good idea, shall we go through to my office." He was an archetypical accountant and he wittered on for ages about the finances of Saint Margaret's. To be honest the finances were irrelevant. I just wanted to see what he was going to let slip. I struggled hard to focus and ask pertinent questions. In a gap in his explanations his wife appeared with more tea and biscuits. A warning look to me was meant to be a hint. What was she trying to tell me? Her husband was in the dark?

"Will you stay to dinner Father?" She made the offer like it was the most natural thing in the world. I had no option. She was definitely trying to tell me something.

"Thank you. I'd be delighted." Well maybe I'd find out something worth knowing. David Brookes talked on and on, oblivious to my growing boredom with the facts and figures. Then again he had a lot to go through and his professionalism was not in question.

As we sat around the table, the three of us, all seemed normal. David, the genial host, talked about everything; from politics to the economy and the social breakdown of society. All the while his wife was giving me tantalising looks and caressing my leg with her stocking covered foot. If I were inclined I could have made her flirting easier and moved forward to enjoy her caresses. It appeared that her husband was oblivious to her extra marital fucking of priests. I hoped it would stay that way.

"Father MacPhail, was an excellent Rector for the parish." David was saying, I looked at him distracted by the rising foot. I nodded my agreement. Trying to concentrate on his words.

"He was a bit of a ladies man, so I hear." Perhaps the wine was loosening his tongue or maybe he knew about his wife's infidelity after all. She however, never even skipped a beat. Her foot teasing as she turned disapproving to her husband.

"David, the man has been murdered for goodness sake." She sounded shocked. Her delivery was flawless and he recoiled a little before her.

"It might have been the reason, you never know." He had a working hypothesis after all. Maybe he was the Hercule Poirot of Gleninch.

"It was a mugging, or so the police have said." I tried to divert everyone. I was learning very little. Perhaps he was about to drop something in my lap. I just hoped it didn't collide with his wife's insistent foot. I am such a tart. A man's a man for a' that as Burns would say.

"I am going out for a cigarette. Do you smoke Father?" He pushed his seat back and stood up. I shook my head. Never did understand why anyone would want to smoke. I just drink instead. One vice less to keep track of.

"Won't be long." He smiled and left me alone with his horny wife. I nodded. She sat there looking like the image of a faithful wife. Loveliness personified.

"He has no idea." She whispered like I understood everything. She was telling me that the treasurer was not in on MacPhail's sins. I wondered if she meant the sex or the Satanism. Going by her actions it was hard to tell. He probably had no idea about any of her extra-curricular activities.

"I see." I looked straight at her, picking up on her arousal. "It might be better if it stays that way."

She smiled, thinking that she would soon be warming my bed as she had warmed MacPhail's. "Where are you staying?" It was hurried now, her husband might be back any second. She wanted the details.

"At the Holiday Inn." This act was working just a little too well. She might end up in my bed and then what the hell would I do. I am not a celibate priest. Oh fuck. Just then the flight of the Valkyrie's began to howl from my phone. I was about to be saved. Saved from myself and the erection that filled my trousers.

"Steel." I answered strongly, looking away from my temptress and placing the phone against my ear. I needed to clear my head quickly.

"Brotherton. We have access to his computer. I thought you might like to come and see what has turned up." He sounded pleased with himself.

"I'll be there in ten minutes." I hung up as my hostess cleared the table and her husband walked in from outside. I quickly made my apologies and left seeking the sanctuary of the Police station. It would, thankfully, keep me busy all night.

Chapter 9

"Well Inspector? What have you found on his computer?" I asked. I knew it had to be juicy or he would have left his call until the morning. Maybe it was just wishful thinking.

"Well, it took a little while to get past the password but that was all that held us back." He paused, sending the constable from the room. He didn't want the facts to leak out. It certainly piqued my interest. A conspiracy was about to be unmasked. Progress was about to be made.

"Why would you put a password on a totally blank computer?" Brotherton's cop mode was in full flow. He looked up from the computer, his face not sitting on the happy spectrum.

"Doesn't make any sense to me. I take it that the computer still has windows on it?" Wow, what a techie I had become. I knew that most PC's used windows but I knew little beyond word and email. It was the telescope all over again.

"It does. But there was nothing else. It has been scrubbed." He spoke with finality, like they had tried everything. I might have used a more industrial description.

"No church records or sermons or anything?" That's what should have been on it. Priests were usually a bit predictable. If nothing was on here then where was it? He certainly didn't have piles of handwritten sermons lying around and Priests don't freestyle every week.

"Not a damn thing. What the hell was he doing?" Brotherton was obviously irritated too. So was I. We were like a pair of wasps caught in a kids jam jar, and someone was shaking us.

"What was his password?" I asked, with no real reason why. I just did. I am always surprised by what comes out of my mouth. It's often a random explosion.

"His password was Jehovah." Brotherton looked at me, missing the irony. What was so unusual about a priest using God's name as his password?

"Really?" Incredulity seeping out. I'll bet the bastard had another computer somewhere. Was this computer left for us to find?

"Seems logical enough to me." Brotherton said. Well, it proved that comprehensive education was successfully producing cultural pygmies, after all. Or perhaps he hadn't been forced to go to Sunday School.

"I doubt that MacPhail would have used THAT as his password. After all he is batting for the other side." I was trying hard not to be dismissive. I had another brainwave. "Can you tell when it was last used? Like a log or something?" Maybe a star-date like the captain's log on Star Trek?

"Maybe." An overwhelming endorsement from Inspector Brotherton. I was touched. His fingers began a tango of love as he did something technical. It looked very impressive to an amateur like me. Menu after menu flashed by as he picked his way to the answer.

"The user account was made yesterday." He looked disgusted. The irritated shove of the keyboard and the accompanying noise matching his expression perfectly.

"What does that mean, exactly?" Trying hard to keep up. I knew what I thought it meant but it was better to check.

"MacPhail has never used this machine. It's been planted to replace the original." He pushed his chair back from the computer and stomped around the room. I could see that the swearing would follow soon.

"Now that is interesting." I meant it. Brotherton stopped his march of the grumpy bastards and looked at me. I don't think interesting was what he thought this was.

"We are so far behind on this case it is ridiculous. Did they really think that I wouldn't notice the machine was a plant. God they must think I am stupid.' His face was a wonderful contortion. Now he was pissed as hell.

"Someone tampered with the scene or swapped it before we were called in." Statements of the obvious never really go wrong. I liked that he was pissed off. I spend most of my life pissed off and it works for me.

"Who? What the fuck is going on?" He might as well have growled at me. Like I knew the answer to that one.

"Let's get some air." I motioned with my head. I didn't want to be overheard. Brotherton was taking a few seconds to catch on. I put my finger to my lips. A silent shh, he got it. We walked out like it was the most natural thing in the world. Two men going outside for a fag. No smoking buildings gave a great excuse to take some air and get some privacy. It wasn't raining but it was cold. Our breath misting as we spoke. We were in a little huddle.

"Who else knows we have the computer?" I had a plan. Perhaps it was even a cunning plan. We needed to use this to our advantage.

"Anyone who looks on the evidence log, the neighbours might have seen us remove it. SOCO and some of the constables here. Why?" He looked at me after a long pull at his cigarette.

"Put in your report that the computer has been examined and nothing was learned from it. Nothing more." He nodded, catching my thinking. A tight little grin beginning to form on his lips.

"We don't need to let them know we know. Someone is fucking with us." Shocked him again. His eyes widening at the F word.

"Who?" His question deserved a good answer. An answer I didn't have. I wanted to have the answer but it would have to wait. We would find out eventually.

"There is a group, of which MacPhail was one, within St Margaret's. They obviously have friends in a few places." I carefully avoided the usual buzz words; sect, cult coven. I didn't want to scare the good inspector.

"Fuck." There, he let it out. Welcome to the F users Club, free memberships available.

"Exactly. I have a lead that I am cultivating. One of MacPhail's bed warmers. Perhaps I can pump her for information." I tried hard not to smirk. Childish and juvenile but I just had to. Brotherton's face split into a smile.

"Pump away. Let me know how it goes." That's my boy, getting into the swing of it. Just because it was serious didn't mean that we couldn't laugh.

"I will, but we need to be careful about what we say. Phones are particularly easy to bug aren't they?" I have seen movies and it looks too easy.

"Yes. Be careful what you say and we will avoid letting anything out. If it is being covered up then they will be watching us." Brotherton stated the obvious beautifully. Our conspiratorial team of two had been born.

"Right then. I will just call your mobile and we can meet up whenever we have anything to discuss. I will report to the Bishop and take over the day to day services at St Margaret's. Time to be vigilant. They will slip up." Confidence filled my voice like I knew what I was talking about.

"Okay. We'll proceed quietly and see what turns up." Brotherton was getting good at agreeing with me. I was beginning to like him. If he kept this up we might even end up friends. I don't have many of those.

"Keep everything to yourself Brotherton, your pension and career might be on the line." He had things to lose that I didn't. He needed to remember that.

"I'll be fine." He sounded like he had felt the heat from above before. Good luck to him this time.

"I am going back to my room, I have to make a report to Bishop Michael. Joy of Joys." I looked heavenward, no inspiration was forthcoming. I think I am meant to help myself.

"Nite then." Brotherton went back inside knowing that he was alone and surrounded by potential spies and enemies. A true Daniel in the lions den. I had a short drive to make to a warm comfortable room. A phone call that loomed large ahead of me. How can I spin out 'I have no idea what is happening on this case.' My whore red car squealed as the fan belt began to slip a little. My little car didn't like the cold and to be honest, I don't like the cold either.

Chapter 10

I plugged the slim plastic card into the slot. I am used to this kind of lock. It came as no surprise when it failed to work first go. A slower attempt and the door unlocked letting me inside. Although not palatial, the room was warm and comfortable. A far cry from some of the budget places I was often sent to. I flicked on the lights and there it was. On the bed, a manilla envelope. It had my name typed on it. Someone had been inside my room and left me a message. I didn't think it was a thank you card from the congregation welcoming me to my temporary stay with them.

I checked the rest of the room before I approached the letter. The shower room and toilet were clean and empty. No psycho moments for me tonight. Shower curtains just give me the creeps. I looked closely at the typing and smiled.

"Dozy bastards." I like my enemies to be able to spell my name at the very least. It brought a smile to my lips to be called Father Steal. I picked the envelope from the bed and peeled it open gently avoiding covering it in finger prints. Well you never know, might yield another clue. After all, the inability to spell might mean that the delivery person was dumb enough to cover it in whorls and whirls. I poured the letter on to the bed and picked it up by a corner.

The letter, on white A4 folded in three sections, was brutal in its simplicity. It had one line across the centre.

"Leave now, you have no place here. Only pain will come to you if you stay." I read aloud. I dropped the letter and envelope on the dresser shelf. Heard it. Got the tee shirt and seen the DVD. Who are these people? They have obviously been watching far too many B-movies. I shook my head and looked in the mirror. It was then I saw the lightest smear, so I huffed on it. The misting on the glass revealed a point of a pentagram. Point down. The twin points upwards representing the horns of Satan. They at least knew that much. Perhaps they were a bit more committed than I had realised.

I checked the bathroom mirror and there was another mark. On the inside of the window another mark had been made. Okay they were pissing me off now. I was beginning to feel the hairs on the back of my neck stand up when I realised that a working had been conducted in my room. There must be other pentagrams one of which would be the focus. If I could find that one I would be able, maybe, to see what the enemy had in store for me. I managed to avoid getting too frantic as I scanned around.

"Fuck, fuck fuckitty fuck!" I was surrounded by little pentagrams. The television had a big one, the bedside lamps a little one each, on the brass plate of the door handle another little five pointer, the metal ceiling lamp had another. This was getting serious. I touched the right hand lamp shade, it's brushed metal surface cold. I got a tingling in my finger tip. I closed my eyes. I tried to see the mark being made, I couldn't. All I could feel was a crowded room. A room full of people with faces I couldn't see.

I searched more thoroughly finding an interesting one on the toilet seat lid and another in the shower. I had lost count of how many there were. I was beginning to feel the net closing in. Everywhere I looked there seemed to be the sign of the horns. The power was growing with each little discovered servant that I found. A tight band was beginning to squeeze my head like a vice. I had to get out of here. Soon or I might be kissing the carpet. I reached the door and realised that the pentagrams weren't random. They had sealed the room. I was trapped in a room of malice. Whoever had laid this trap was a sorcerer and not an apprentice either. I could not get out. The door, windows and even the water way from the loo were sealed. I could feel my gorge rising. I was going to vomit my dinner all over the place. Oh the embarrassment. I made it to the sink only to see the taps caressed with a star. Too bad, my mouth was filling with saliva, without water it was inevitable. My head thudding as the grip of the vice made me feel dizzy and weak, I closed my eyes and let go. I made most of it hit the sink, not in the sink but in that general area. The rest went into the toilet. The splash radius was contained but some splattered the bottom of my trousers and my shoes. The retching and coughing went on for a few minutes as I tried to get my equilibrium back. My nose had delivered a fountain of it's own and the residual smell was making me want to retch again. I blew my nose hard and the remaining sickness sprayed across the tiled floor. Almost in the style of a professional footballer. I almost laughed, but not quite. I needed to get out. Hysteria was beginning to want its moment.

The phone. I staggered to the bedside phone, it was adorned too. They had been very thorough and I was beginning to feel the panic pulling at me. Now that I knew I was inside the seals of my enemy to touch the pentagrams would probably make me pass out. Sometimes there are downsides to feeling things. A vibration in my pocket pulled my mind into focus. A fucking text. I put my hand in my pocket and pulled out my mobile. My salvation was from Korea. Samsung had saved the day. I dialled the front desk and asked for some assistance. The night porter said he would be along immediately.

I stood staring at the door waiting. It was all I could do to keep the room from swirling round me. It was like I was drunk as the room canted from side to side. I held my head together with both hands, one at each temple. The door opened and a very confused young man asked me if I was all right.

'I need another room.' I managed as I got into the hall. 'I have been sick all over the bathroom. I am sorry, it was something I ate.' He looked at me sceptically, but led me to another room down the hall. The poor guy would have to clean it up. He brought me a key-card a few minutes later.

'Do you need a doctor?' I obviously didn't look very healthy. I shook my head and waved him away as nicely as I could manage. He deposited my bags inside and left me to it. The pain in my skull was lessening, thankfully. There would be a reckoning for this. Anger filled me taking over from the fear I had felt just moments ago.

I staggered to the window and opened it. It barely opened, just in case I was prone to jumping. It is only the first floor for goodness sake. I needed air. Clean, cold fresh air. I stood like a gasping fish drinking in the cure to my malady. I looked down at my vomit decorated trousers and shoes. Very tastefully done. I needed a shower. My report would need to wait a little while. Making a call to Bishop Michael needed working up to. Besides he was probably in bed by now. It was past eleven and I was about to disturb my neighbours by standing in the shower until I used all the hot water. Too bad, my need was greater than theirs. Bite me.

Chapter 11

It's like a hangover for me. When I get too much stimulation the next morning can be a little difficult. Add to that projectile vomit and a sense of danger and I am in for a fragile morning. I didn't set the alarm, preferring the organic method of waking up. Bladder pressure is the limiting factor and eventually it will wake me up.

"House keeping." A cheery female voice reached my ears. I managed not to be offensive, I think, when I sent back the 'later' response. The heavy curtains had kept the room quite dark. Probably just as well as I had strewn my stuff about in my efforts to recover from my incident.

I rolled over thinking that I could escape back to a dreamless sleep and a long lie in bed. No rest for the wicked apparently. Buzzing and ringing my mobile phone began its call for attention. It wasn't that early, but it still pissed me off. I picked it up and looked disgustedly at my saviour of last evening. On the display it was Bishop Michael. I'd better answer it then.

"Steel." A winner of a start. A bit neutral not really giving too much away.

"Andrew, how are things in Gleninch?" He was such a morning person. At least he had waited until nearly ten. This was late by his standards.

"Well, things are progressing I think." Master of the say fuck all, that I am. I took a deep breath but Bishop Michael beat me to the next bit.

"In what way?" He wasn't letting me flannel him today. He still sounded relatively cheerful. That would be changing soon I thought.

"I don't know what is going on. I have, however, had a threatening phone call and a mystical attack on me in my hotel room. Oh yes and a warning letter.' I paused. I like to get things out in the open early.

"That sounds dangerous. Are you all right? How about your police assistance? Is it forthcoming?" Way to go a bombardment of questions. I took a breath.

"It is. Yes. The police inspector I have assigned is a good man, considering there is evidence of a bit of pressure to hush the lot up." Conspiracy theory too, what a delivery from me. The hits they keep on coming.

"Keep your eyes open Andrew. I have made arrangements for you to take over at Saint Margaret's for the coming weeks till we clear this up." The Bishop's desk phone started to ring. It was time to let him get on with running things.

"I will be fine. I'll call in later today. This looks like a long one." Tell him what he wants to hear.

"Okay Andrew I'll speak to you soon. Be careful." And a final click and he was off the line. No hanging about with Bishop Michael.

"Thanks for your call. Bollocks." I was well and truly awake now. I staggered to the toilet trying to get my fuzzy head to function. I popped a couple of aspirin and swigged from the tap. After an extended seat in the bathroom I got dressed. Jeans and a baggy sweat shirt, I would be in plain clothes for the day. I needed to get my official uniform cleaned. Oh the joys. I might even need a new one, I would be so embarrassed putting it in to be cleaned.

After an extended apology and offers of financial restitution I was able to keep my room at the inn. No stables out the back. It had been a little embarrassing trying to feign food poisoning as the reason for the projectile vomit. I know that priests have a reputation for the imbibing curse of whisky. I have been known occasionally to hit the bottle with a vengeance. I am sure the manager was thinking that I was of the alcoholic brotherhood. Too bad, I wasn't going to try and change his mind. Someone here had allowed access to my room. It might even have been him so I just let it go and went out.

I migrated to the heart of the matter, the white church that was Saint Margaret's in the fields. I was a nice church for its type. Well, it was in decent nick at any rate. I had been here on a few occasions; most notably school Christmas carol services. It was close to my old high school, a place that was a source of torment for those of academic persuasion, unless of course, you were good at sports too. I was naturally disinterested in sports and made little effort to get involved with the Luddites that wanted to kick my head in. Well, I had no interest in a return visit for old time's sake.

I opened the doors, which were unlocked, like every house of god should be. I always like the feeling of being alone in a church. It is like a warm familiar blanket that surrounds you, making you feel safe. I needed that, this morning, especially after last night's escapades. I sat on the front pew, with its crocheted kneelers and heated panel. Devotion to God need not be uncomfortable in the winter. The heating wasn't on at the moment but the cold air wasn't too upsetting. I knelt and let myself pray. It is more like a meditation experience as I let my brain wander after I give thanks and beg forgiveness for the sins I have and am about to commit. I have a very personal arrangement with the almighty, and it seems to work well for us both. It is simply a no blame culture. I don't criticise his actions and he doesn't blast me into oblivion with lightning strikes. I don't push my luck too far though, just in case.

It was while I was kneeling at prayer that I heard the outer door being opened and soon I had company in the pews. I looked round, a middle aged woman had joined me near the front. I nodded to her and smiled. It was returned after she crossed herself and settled down to pray.

After about ten minutes I left her to her reflection and went into the vestibule. I was looking over the church notices when she emerged. Her eyes were a little moist. A sadness had settled on her features, she obviously had a burden to carry.

"Are you looking for someone?" She asked politely. I obviously didn't look like I should have been there. I smiled to her. I decided that levity was not the right response in this case.

"I am Father Andrew Steel. I will be covering here for a while until a replacement can be found for Father MacPhail. Pleased to meet you." I extended a hand and she took it. Nothing happened thankfully. I could feel her sadness, didn't need to be a psychic to do that. Sometimes normal is what I need.

"Christine McLeod. I am pleased to meet you too, Father." Her smile was one that had more than a tinge of relief. I could have been anybody. A member of the press, a vagrant or just the psycho who had killed their Priest. After all I wasn't exactly dressed for the part.

"Would you like a cup of tea?" I can be taught. She accepted and looked like she needed to share with someone. A stranger would be just perfect. I doubted that MacPhail would have been much help to her. Maybe I was wrong. In a few minutes we were ensconced in soft seats like old friends as she began to tell me her tale of woe.

Her son, John, was on active service in Iraq. She was terrified and could barely watch the news. It was filled with bombings and deaths, and increasingly hostile news coverage about the legitimacy of the war. She was fraught and her nerves were frazzled. He was due home in a few weeks and while she was glad of that, she felt a mounting panic that something terrible was going to happen. It always seemed that fate cruelly snatched those on their way back to loved ones. She carried the worry that all service families do, but for her John was all she had left. Long divorced her son filled her thoughts.

I let her speak for a while until she ran out steam. I made all the right noises and then asked her about the congregation. She was relatively alone in the church, surrounded by those who never really took the time to include her. She had been coming for almost two years but still felt totally isolated. I got the impression that MacPhail was too busy for real pastoral care. How many others had he neglected as he fornicated in his little coven. My face grew a frown. My face often gives me away , a direct line to my thoughts.

"I've said too much Father I am sorry." She began to

apologise. I stopped her with a smile and reassurances that I had just remembered that I was to go to the police station this morning. I really wanted her to be okay and I let my sincerity escape like a beam of goodwill.

"I hope you will come on Sunday. It will be nice to see a familiar face." I wanted her to be comforted in her time of need. She seemed to accept my excuse, but the time was over and she had to go too. Perhaps I needed a little reminder of what was and what wasn't the lord's work. We left together. A communion of sorts.

Chapter 12

MacPhail's funeral was not mine to officiate over. There are limits to my hypocrisy and that would have been one step too far. I did, however, attend the service at 'the Crem.' It was the crematorium in the nearby town of Kirkcaldy. A simple service with three hymns and a few readings. The singing was particularly tuneless. I did think the turnout for the service was quite good. There appeared to be a good mix of family, friends and parishioners. I wondered how many had been intimate with the man in the coffin and how many were part of whatever was going on. I sat at the back and watched. Once or twice I caught a few sidelong looks in my direction. The plot thickened before my eyes. A collection was made for a charity supporting missionary work in Africa. I didn't want to support his message being exported.

As the final tortured verse of 'Abide with me' was being completed I looked at those who sat nearest the front. They were my prime suspects. The blessing sent us all on our way. After a few silent moments of reflection that I used to think of what I might say in response to any questions that came my way we were told of a buffet lunch being held at the Salazar hotel further into Kirkcaldy. I looked up and caught the eye of Angela Brookes. A mischievous smile almost made it to her face as she winked to me. I could feel my ears beginning to heat up. That was most definitely a problem in the making.

"Good morning Father." Angela let her presence be known as we moved from the hand shaking line to the car park. I had expected to get some sort of indications from the line up but I didn't. Of course the pain and loss that filled the Crematorium had been laid down by thousands, if not millions, of mourners over the years. I thought I might have been able to escape without the Complication that had just called out to me.

"Angela, lovely to see you." I managed to smile. Not a hint of salaciousness in tone or face for that matter. I was in public and didn't need a hint of scandal this early in the day. She, however, was an expert at clandestine flirting. Her eyes flashed intent as she made a seemingly simple request. She was a good looking woman.

"Can you give me a lift to the Salazar? David dropped me off for the service. He had to work today. He was so disappointed." All sorts of information had just been passed. She looked very tidy today, make up understated, clothes giving no hint of the, undoubtedly, sexy lingerie that was hidden underneath. Perhaps I was projecting what I hoped was hidden.

"Of course, no problem at all." I was committed now. If she was involved, I was heading for trouble. If she wasn't then she was simply a sex mad adulteress who fucked priests as her partner of choice. Oh the sins I would probably be committing. I led her over to the red chariot that waited unobtrusively in the car park. I could almost feel the tension in the air as we got to the car. Even the clunk-kitty click of the central locking felt anticipatory. A moment later we were inside and buckled in. I had no idea what to say. Like I said, I am not great at small talk.

"Do you know how to get there? The Salazar, that is?" Angela asked. I replied in the negative, although I knew where it was. It would keep her busy until we got there. Perhaps it might prevent things getting out of hand on the way. Not that my fantasies were getting to the surface of my brain.

"I make much better tea than the Salazar. Do you want to come back to mine for some?" She said it like she was discussing the weather. Damn she was good.

"Sounds like a better idea." I was in, deep. I didn't actually care. The prospect of sex with this, rather fine, woman was the over riding thought. She smiled a wicked little smile. She had me and she knew it. Worse still, I knew it too. I started the car and in a few moments we were driving towards Gleninch and an illicit encounter that I, certainly, would never forget. You can't be led anywhere you don't really want to go.

As I drove I was checking her out. She was a pretty thirty something. Not perfect by any means but a woman a man would be proud to have on his arm. She had great legs and had regained her figure after the birth of her one child. Her eyes were a greeny-blue augmented by mascara and eye shadow that showed them beautifully. I liked what I saw. I was on tenterhooks as I drove along, expecting a caressing hand to reach for my loins. I was disappointed and the journey passed without any inappropriate actions. After a battery of small talk about the service I pulled up outside the Brookes' house. It looked so ordinary looking, a priest dropping off a member of his congregation and coming in for a cup of tea. The reality would be so different.

She walked up the path and unlocked the door, welcoming me to her house. I wondered how it would go. I, after all, am not MacPhail; maybe she liked her priest to take charge and treat her badly. Punishment scenarios that sort of thing. If that was what she liked I was fucked, literally. I can play along but I have no idea how that sort of thing goes.

"Just milk isn't it Father?" She called from the kitchen as she clicked the kettle on. Maybe I was imagining too much. She came to the kitchen doorway and smiled sexily. Leaning against the door frame and managing not to look like a clique or a bunny boiler.

"Or should we just skip the tea?" I tried to look unsurprised but failed to pull it off. I tried to smile back but probably looked scared. She walked slowly towards me and kissed my lips gently. Taking my hand she led me upstairs. I should have resisted but I didn't really want to. I hadn't had sex for months, at least, not the kind that involved someone else. She looked delicious as she led me up the staircase. Her bedroom looked so very normal. This was anything but.

Its not that I haven't had sex in the daytime with a married woman before. It is simply that I haven't done it with someone who could easily be on the other side. I know that it was stupid and totally lust driven, but it was damn good. All my worries about her desire for kinky sex were unfounded. She was simply a very sexual woman who got off knowing she was fucking her priest. Deep rooted issues I think. I managed reasonably well, I think, considering it had been so long. I left after about two hours giving her time to tidy up and make like nothing had taken place in her marital bed. I went back to the Holiday Inn and showered. The hot water was so very welcome. I noticed that my cheeks were ruddy and I looked younger. Amazing, one good session and the years fall off. From inside the room my phone was calling me to action.

"Steel." I almost sounded cheerful. I'd better stop that

before anyone thought I had been replaced by a doppelgänger

"That's much better." It was Angela. Her voice seemed much huskier than I remembered it being. However, that wasn't what I had been paying attention to.

"Hi, everything okay?" I asked her, a little too quickly. Worry clutching my gut that I had been compromised and the fan was about to be covered in the brown stuff.

"Couldn't be much better. Thank you for today. Anytime you feel like dropping by just drop me a text. I can't wait." She spoke like a naughty teenager. Maybe she was. I was joining in.

"I had a great time too. Thank you." I have no idea what to say in these situations. There is no real protocol for it in the Canon Code.

"Gotta go. I will send you something as a reminder. Later." She was gone just like that. I was surprised and I sat down on the bed, the towel round my waist parting to reveal the only part of me that had been thinking today. I shook my head in disappointment at myself. The phone rang again.

"Steel." I still didn't sound like the grumpy man that usually answered my phone.

"Brotherton, can you come down?" He sounded a bit put out. He wouldn't be saying any more over the phone.

"Of course, I'm just out of the shower but won't be too long." I wondered what he wanted. Hopefully something had come up.

You never know. It might even be a clue.

"Father Steel, I am glad you could make it." Inspector Brotherton met me in the car park. He was still smoking a cigarette. He looked irritated and it wasn't my fault this time.

"No problem. Developments?" I asked quietly. He nodded. I could have been saying anything if we were being watched. I am not that clear a speaker at times and prone to the odd mumble.

"We have a confession. He is sitting in the cells right now. Claims it was a burglary that went wrong and that he didn't mean to kill the priest." Disgusted Brotherton flicked the butt of his cigarette away. It bounced a few times before rolling to a remnant of yesterday's rain. There were always puddles to be found in Gleninch. It lies right in the rain passage of Fife, planners eh?

"Really, wow. Has he managed to keep his story straight?" Fake confessions wasted a great deal of police time. I tried not to swear and succeeded, a whole new me.

"He has the details and a murder weapon. Looks like a closed case. At least that's what the Fiscal's office is calling it. We're done." He looked me in the eye. His face holding a blank look that wouldn't give him away.

"You know that its bollocks, and so do I." I paused, "I have to get to the bottom of the situation at St Margaret's regardless of the Procurator Fiscal's office. I might need your help anyway."

"I'll do what I can but I'm being reassigned to another case tomorrow. We are six for six on murders this year." Brotherton didn't like the smell of it either. A confession would mean his talents would be allocated elsewhere and I was going to be on my own for the most part.

"I got a threatening letter trying to scare me off, and a call. Best keep our eyes open. This isn't over by a long way." Brotherton's eyebrows shot up in response. He was surprised at my calmness, I expect.

"Be careful Father, this is a dangerous town." His tone telling me that I had no real idea how dangerous it had become.

"Oh I will. I am always careful." A bravado that I didn't really feel filling my voice. I left him then. I didn't need to meet the patsy. He would get off with manslaughter and out in a few short years. Who was he hiding? Fucked if I knew, yet.

Chapter 13

"The blood of Christ, given for you." I tipped the chalice forward, a little wine passed the lips of the elderly woman kneeling at the rail. Her stick was protruding past the rail and I stepped around it, carefully. Repeating my phrase as I delivered the communion wine to all comers to the feast of Christ. They had already had the wafers that some felt had been transformed into the actual body of Christ. This was my first Sunday service at St Margaret's Only the prayer and dismissal to go. I was determined to depart from the norms and have a special prayer for those who risked their lives for their country. A few eyebrows would rise at that.

"Go in peace to love and serve the Lord." I sang out and the joyous flock sang back the response "In the name of Christ, Amen." And my ordeal was over. Only the coffee morning to navigate and it would be over. A grateful look came my way from Christine McLeod, it was all worth it. I had carefully avoided too many looks at Angela, she was a disaster in progress. I didn't need to make it obvious.

I took a deep breath as I removed my outer robes and made

my way to the door. Hand shaking and 'lovely to see you's ' to go. No feelings flooding me as I took their hands. Some limp, some firm, some clammy and all of them on their way out the house of God.

A few moments later I was accepting the plaudits of a wonderful sermon from an old bloke who had served his country in the War, I didn't ask which one. The procession of faces that had disappeared out the door left only the hardiest of core congregation members inside having coffee. It seemed strange to me that so many had left, I had expected more to stay. Maybe all had not been so great after all. Perhaps the outsiders just didn't feel welcome here. Lord knows I didn't feel welcome either. I walked in to a hall full of conversation. It missed a beat, almost.

Maybe I am a bit paranoid. Here am I, Daniel in the lion's den, about to chat and glad-hand my way through a nest of vipers. Some of those in this room are definitely involved in some sort of supernatural naughtiness. Maybe I should just make my own coffee. Some of the faces I recognised, some I didn't. Didn't appear to be that many kids around today.   I would have expected to see more of them. Still maybe they'll come to the youth club tonight. No doubt I'd find out.

"Lovely sermon this morning, Father.'" A white haired, well turned out elderly gentleman grasped my hand and shook it vigorously. His eyes sparkled a little too much for my liking, why I have no idea. I didn't think it was that moving. I had slipped in a few double entendres that might have given an impression to the shadow flock that I was one of them. Maybe that was what had made him well up? I nodded conspiratorially, but didn't want to be too obvious. Quicksand all around.

"Coffee Father?" David Brookes extended a brown liquid filled white cup. His other hand held his own. They say that if you need milk and sugar in coffee then you don't actually like it. The bitter taste that met my lips questioned my belief that I liked coffee. David smiled as my face registered the taste. He was the only one I knew wasn't on their side, and I was shagging his wife.

"It takes some getting used to. It is amazing what you can get used to." He began to steer me to a table with some other middle aged professional types. You know pillars of the community and all that. I wondered about them, they were probably safe-ish.

"I'd like to introduce you to the Thursday night gang." It was obviously an in thing. The explanation of their weekly card game and an informal invite to come and lose my money were forthcoming.

"With my poker playing skills I would lose my stipend in no time at all." We laughed together. I noticed a little symbol in some spilled sugar on the table. It was slowly wiped away by John something, I really should pay attention. It was a funny little loopy squiggle that I was meant to recognise. I nodded slowly while catching his eye and moving on to another group. Another one identified in this motley crew.

"How are you settling in Father?" An elderly lady fired from across another table. There was a whole gallery of them sipping from cups and jibber jabbering to each other. I had no idea which one fired at me but I smiled and professed that I had been made most welcome and was very pleased to be here. I told them all how nice the Holiday Inn was, I can fib a little.

I can feel my spidey senses going off all round me as eyes are following me round the room. Acting as natural as I can, I try to scope out the congregation and split them into them and not them. Thankfully, I am just about finished the first chalice of brown cooling sludge. There appears to have been a thinning out of the coffee drinkers and only a few remain, including Angela Brookes. Her Husband is busy and her daughter is talking animatedly with her friend Hannah, when Angela gives me a look that would give a statue an erection. I look away quickly hoping no one has noticed. She is an expert at this surreptitious flirting. I am out of my league. I turn in time to be approached by a middle aged man, whom I have been introduced to, whose name is a blank.

"Father, it is a pleasure to have you with us at such an important time." He speaks quietly but not a whisper. Another one, perhaps? I add him to the mental list of Them.

"I serve wherever I am needed." I go for cryptic and

ambiguous. I leave my face schooled and give nothing away. Or at least I hope I pull it off.

"And you are needed here. Welcome to our little group." He pats me on the shoulder as he makes his way from the hall. Like all Churches the same few do the tidying up and putting away. In St Margaret's it seems it is the Brookes's turn on the rota. I make my goodbye's and escape before I get into any more trouble. One last look from Angela was worth it. Smokinnn.

Chapter 14

"Andrew, how are things….progressing?" Bishop Michael was always so circumspect when he had to call. I hadn't been checking in regularly enough, obviously. Progress would be an overstatement. I knew that there were bad guys here and they knew I knew. Other than that there was 'eff all progress made in the last week. I couldn't pretend otherwise.

"Slowly Bishop, slowly." I paused, I like to irritate him if he calls, rebel that I am.

"Such as? Any more threats?" Since they hexed my room at the inn, all had been quiet. I'm not complaining either. I didn't need another night like that. Ever.

"No, fortunately. Anything on the star charts?" It's a bit like tennis, our conversations. I am more a John McEnroe style player or I'd like to be. The bishop is a steadier Swedish style. Maybe a Borg or an Edberg.

"I will have something for you tomorrow. It has our friends in a bit of a tizzy. They are very interested, can you make it over tomorrow around four?" It wasn't really a request and we both knew it. I know a summons when I get one.

"Of course, I'll see you then." Dismissive compliance at its best, could just have said 'whatever'. I didn't let out my inner teenager.

"Andrew, be careful." He sounded worried and that was a rarity in itself. What did the old fox know that he didn't want to say over the phone? I would find out in his time and no other. Not that he was a control freak or anything. He could just have spit it out and saved me a trip.

"I will." Click, check up call over. No blood spilled, no arguments; just a passive-assertive 'Get a move on!' I glower at the keypad of my phone and drop it with a sour look into my jacket pocket. I am on my way to dispense communion to a few of the older, house-bound members of the congregation and then a hospital visit. Probably explains my grumpiness, either that or I am generally a miserable sod. If I were a celibate I'd blame my moodiness on that. However, in the last week, I have had more rumpy-pumpy than in the last two years so that most certainly isn't the problem. I think I am looking younger.

As if in response to my thoughts, my phone vibrates. 'Answer me' it seems to scream. I frown and fumble about until I look at the small screen. A text, all that for a bloomin text. It is more than a text, a full graphic close up of Angela Brook's bits; and a come and get me message. The woman knows she can have me any time and I need to put a stop to this and soon. It is so getting out of hand. I'm not that great at it, I'd say she is though. A smirk covers my face as I look at the picture, again, and text back 'On my way'. I told you, I am a bit stupid at times. A spring in my step in anticipation of a brief social interlude and I am underway in no time.

Angela Brookes, is stamped with a health warning. Or at least she should be. I know I should not be in her bed, lying back as she gives me the most toe curling sensations. Under the duvet her mouth is trying to give me the punishment heart-attack that I deserve. I push away the duvet and see her in all her luscious glory working up and down me. How beautifully decadent; her red lipstick and perfect white teeth almost hypnotic as she relishes my flesh. In the middle ages she'd have been burned at the stake as a succubus and a temptress. In this century she's just a bored housewife with a thing for priests. Progress.

A sunny Sunday post Eucharist tumble is certainly not how I expected this day to go. I didn't resist, even though I might indeed be sleeping with the enemy. How deep was she in? probably right up to my neck. I know that MacPhail had certainly enjoyed her sinful wiles. Why on earth didn't that stop me? Like I said, stupidity shouldn't be ruled out.

I am pulled back into the here and now as she has released me temporarily and climbed aboard. Tight, hot, wet and energetic I am drowning in a sea of her making. Time flies past and soon I am kissing her goodbye. An unforgettable experience, hopefully it won't get me killed. I whistle softly to myself as I head out to take communion to the elderly. The sun is smiling down on me. Either that or God is glaring at me.

Gleninch is a town of roundabouts; they provide a level of entertainment and conflict between those who know which lane to be in and the idiots who don't. I happen to know which is which, being a native. I was, however, distracted by a ten foot Tyrannosaurus Rex that was meant to pass as roadside art emerging from the foliage in the middle of one. So I went round again like a tourist. Not the sort of thing you see everyday. Although Gleninch has hippopotamus cast from concrete scattered around the place. I don't think it is hippopotami, might be wrong though.

The flashing blue lights that caught my attention moments later didn't prepare me for what came next. The local traffic police were pulling me over. Oh the shame, tourist driving gets you pulled over and me a born a bred native.

"Is there a problem officer?" Why do we all say that? "No, I want your autograph" isn't going to be the response is it. Well maybe for some it might be.

"Step out of the car and turn off the engine please, sir" No nonsense, he might well have added. His tone was officious, if I am being kind, intimidating if I'm not. I look like a problem motorist of course, a bit stubbly (I shaved in a hurry this morning after I slept in), hair as usual and a dog-collar. Priests are such bad boys.

I do as the nice officer asks and reach in my pocket for my ID. He looks like he wants to hit me with his night stick. It usually takes time for me to illicit this level of hostility. Did I piss this one off at the crime scene? I don't think so but who knows. I do it so often and indiscriminately.

"Ease down, I'm just getting my Id." I'm trying to diffuse the situation for a change. He doesn't present the 'protect and serve' persona; more a 'I'm gonna kick your head in' one reserved for Saturday nights.

"I know who you are. This is your third warning" he's moving forward, his voice low and full of menace. "We are watching you. Its time you just left. This is none of your affair. Understand?" He is in close now and it looks like he wants to hit me. He's fervent, all shiny eyes and barely hanging on. No numbers on his epaulettes either. Needs a mint, too.

"I hear you." I manage to stay calm. He's within head-butting range and I have nowhere to step back to. This might get very painful. I prepare for the inevitable.

"You and your chums can fuck right off." Great line eh? I

never know what is going to escape my lips at moments of tension. Apparently the head butt that I expect turns out to be a knee in the groin and I am kissing the tarmac as his boot caresses by ribs. Air is in very short supply as I gasp like a landed fish. The shooting pains coursing through me are almost unbearable.

"You've been warned Fucker." He stomps back to the traffic car and the warning has well and truly been delivered. I manage to pull myself up and back into my car. Excruciating pain filling my core and bile rising in my gorge. My ribs feel like they don't want to expand as I try to get air into my lungs. The burning sensation brings tears to my eyes, that and the crushing pain from my groin. I don't know whether to rub them or count them, if you take my meaning.

Chapter 15

"Body of Christ, given for you." I practically stuff the wafer into her mouth. I need to concentrate. I keep thinking about earlier. Her croaky 'Amen' the prompt for me to proffer the chalice and present it to her lips. The salvation giving body and blood of Christ has passed her lips.

Communion for the infirm and elderly can take a large chunk of time. I had already brought solace and nurture to three old souls and had a hospital visit to follow this one. Being the parish priest is a busy job, how did MacPhail manage it with all the extra-curricular activities he was engaged in? No idea but I was running about like a headless chicken. Perhaps the post-Eucharist tumble should have been avoided.

"The Blood of Christ, given for you." At least she was ready this time. I gave her the contents and tidied up my things. Her eyes closed as she prayed. I suppose its natural to be closer to God the closer one gets to going.

A blessing to conclude and I am ready to go. The ache in the pit of my stomach is still there, but subsiding, and the tenderness of my ribs growing. I just want to get finished so I can self medicate with Glenfiddich. At least it will help me sleep. Just the hospital to go. It was this last stop that I dreaded most. Bedside manner is not my thing; I never know what to say. Long pauses, usually uncomfortable, and banal blethering about the weather or the news fill hospital visits. Trying to sit for any length of time will be excruciating.

A polite refusal of a cup of tea and I reach the sanctuary of my car. No flat tyres, no broken windscreen, no key-scratches and no further warnings then.

The Queen Mary General Hospital, as it was in my day has changed beyond all recognition. What once was a forbidding old building of dubious design has been transformed into an architectural modern beauty of glass and steel. Of course, in Fife, all the investment goes into Kirkcaldy and not Gleninch but it doesn't stop me admiring the building. A multi-storey car park to the rear with lots of spaces and clear signs directing non-locals where they need to go has replaced the old gravel park that passed as parking in years gone by. Although it is dark, it is busy with lots of coming and going. Visiting time is flexible these days, apparently.

Following the new blue signs, which are easy to see and understand, I find myself at ward Nine, post surgery convalescence. How helpful they even tell you what the ward is for. No starchy Sisters or Matrons but a helpful receptionist who smiling asks me who I am here to visit. Luckily I remember without referring to my scrap of paper. Jimmy Anderson, not the cricketer, has a visitor – me. It is logged in the register. All very efficient, I am directed to his room. Room! All of the patients have their own private room. The NHS has come a long way from the four-bed common spaces of the past with the pull round drapes. Money well spent if you ask me. Privacy and dignity when you are ill, not being on show to the whole world.

Jimmy Anderson is around sixty, grey hair and of a basically sour looking demeanour. Grumpy would probably do. Mind you, if I had just my liver transplanted then I might be a tad crabbit too. Very little jaundice and he looks like it might have been a success. Liver failure is a terrible thing, I've seen a few taken in the past. It is not the way to go.

"Mr Anderson, I'm Father Steel. I'm Father MacPhail's replacement." I smile (well twitch my face a bit) and extend my hand. His other hand has a drip connected but his handshake is firm enough. He isn't leaving this mortal coil anytime soon; he is too stubborn I expect. Hale is how he might have been described in years gone by.

"Pleased to meet you father. Terrible business, MacPhail, I mean." His face gives nothing away. I try not to give much away either. Although the throbbing inside has me a little off my game.

"Indeed, the congregation is still reeling at the shock of it. His funeral was a lovely service." Black tongue time has commenced. Will I burn in hell for lying? No, I only lie to the bad guys, honest.

"So, how are you holding up?" I venture, a little sympathetically but in a manly way. It's a start. I don't think he wants the soft soap, syrupy stuff that some need.

"My back is killing me but other than that I'm fine." He isn't comfortable with talking about it, I can tell. Oh well, I plough on anyway.

"You'll be up and around in no time I expect." I'm doing my best but the ache from my nether regions is reminding me of its existence. I shift uncomfortably on the hard plastic chair. Visiting time may be flexible but I can't imagine visitors sitting on this for an hour; sore bollocks or no.

"I bloody hope so." He grumbles giving away nothing. He shifts on the bed, it probably isn't any more comfortable than the chair.

"I have communion with me, if you'd like." I say this in as ambiguous a fashion as possible, looking for a clue that may or may not be there. Baiting the hook.

"Ours or theirs?" He winks a little humour lightening up his crabbit features. Bingo, he's one of the opposition. A slow reeling in needed, I might even get something useful.

"Only ours." I wink as I say it. I hope they just take a wafer and don't have special phrases to say, or I am well screwed. Hoist by my own petard, as it were.

He nods as I reach into my pilot case. I fumble about before coming up with a bit of a holy wafer, hoping that they use the same one's as I do. I put my finger to my lips, in a keep quiet signal. I surreptitiously look over my shoulder to the door as I lean forward to deliver the wafer into his mouth. Cleverly I try to keep it out of his line of sight. I think I've managed to pull it off. He swallows it quickly.

"Curse the Nazarene." He whispers. He's bought my cover. I have a positive ID on another one of the enemy. Another one down loads to go, no doubt. He closes his eyes to savour his unholy communion, a tight smile of satisfied rebellion on his face. I want to punch him. Probably better not.

My phone vibrates and buzzes in my pocket. Maybe I can escape without giving myself away after all. I frown, letting myself look irritated at the interruption and then raise my eyebrows in apology. My hand fumbling into my pocket.

"No rest for the wicked eh?" Anderson manages to croak out, a small smile playing on his lips. His yellowy stained teeth creeping into view. Years of nicotine sticks have left their mark on him. His fingers bearing similar mementoes of his habit.

"Apparently." I manage to look like I was in on his

witticism. It's obvious I am going to leave and I close up my case and pull on my jacket. Anderson wants to ask something. Something delicate I expect as he beckons me forward. I lean in, hoping he's going to drop another gem for me. His voice low and gravelly he drops the bomb.

"Father, this was a white liver wasn't it? I was promised a white liver. I don't want any dirty black's organs in me. Not for twenty thousand I don't." His grip on my sleeve is fervent. His eyes searching mine looking for the reassurance he needs.

"Relax, all is as you requested. Get well and I'll see you soon." I extricate myself smoothly and leave him with a gentle pat on the shoulder. He leans back against the white pillows with the blue 'property of' peeking out.

"Dark is the way." He whispers waving me away. Time for a quick exit. I close the door behind me and leave, with more clues than I know what to do with. It is like doing a jigsaw from the back with no picture.

What on earth was that old goat on about? Didn't want a black liver? Like I knew what he meant. It was like a secret I was supposed to know. I must have bluffed well enough because he seemed to accept my words.

"A black liver?" I muse out loud; sometimes it helps, not often but you never know when it will. It's my excuse for talking to myself and I'm sticking to it.

"A black liver?" Just in case I wasn't listening to myself or didn't hear first time. I am pacing around my generic motel room, whisky glass in my hand and my bollocks still aching. It really isn't big enough to pace being about six steps by about four steps. It is beginning to bug me, I am asking the right question but have no idea what the answer is.

When in doubt put the telly on. After all, noise seems to help me think. Honestly, it does. I don't think well in silence. Anyway, BBC news 24 is a good choice, I can argue with the news presenters. Has anyone noticed that there are always two of them nowadays? Changed days. Is it now an anchor couple rather than the anchor man?

After sections on the economy, which I don't understand, and a section on the Royal family about whom I don't care. The sport is due up after a special report on Africa. It's a load of drivel about changes due to charitable relief and Medicin-sans-frontiers. It did, however, make me watch for a moment and in that moment, I get an idea. A terrible idea about MacPhail and his nasty little cult. He went to Africa every year. Collections were made for a village in wherever the fuck was it. Damn, I couldn't remember.

"It's about organs!" I blurt to myself. A smirk plays across my lips as I think the double entendre. Juvenile, yep, sorry. "So that's where the black liver's comes in."

Of course I have no idea how they do it but at least I have a working theory, (a first), which needs to be looked at. It's too late to call Brotherton with my revelation.

Chapter 16

About four, Bishop Michael had said, so four on the dot is what he meant. A very precise man, the Bishop. So five past four saw me pulling in to the neat grey gravel drive and parking my red smear next to the four black cars that were parked neatly in a row. A rose among thorns.

The Bishop's mansion is a very grand affair, not exactly a mansion but more a manor house large and solidly built. The lintel stone bears the Roman numerals for the eighteenth century, a time when buildings were made to last. The double doors are oak studded with iron and you wouldn't want to try to shoulder them in. A good first-line of defence from the days of angry mobs. Scars in the stones on either side evidence of the past.

Clunk-kitty-clunk and I stuff my keys back into my pocket. I have made an effort, though. I have shaved, have clean clothes on, polished my shoes and brushed my hair. My dog collar is nice and white. I am, after all, staying to dinner. Gravel crunching under my feet as I approach the door and, as if by magic, it opens. Magic in the form of a young priest, standing aside and waiting for my entry. Aren't they getting younger these days?

"Welcome Father Andrew. His Eminence is ready for you, in the Library." He smiles but it doesn't reach his eyes, like a server in McDonalds. I smile back with a similar lack of sparkle.

"I know the way, thank you." I hand him my coat, even though he didn't ask. Butler training is not what it once was, apparently. His smile evaporates; obviously no-one told him that he was the butler. Still, better a butler than being a lackey. I hear the heavy door close behind me as I walk smartly along the corridor to the library. I ignore the portraits of previous residents, their disapproval not needed today. I knock, a little too, forcibly on the door.

"Come in." Authority voice being projected, he obviously has an audience to impress. I smirk inwardly 'If he has on the full regalia I will wet myself.' A little twinkle settles in my eyes as I go in. There is humour everywhere, if only one looks for it.

"Andrew, so glad you could make it. Come in, come in." He seems in a good mood. Too much sherry, perhaps, his cheeks are a little ruddier than I expected. Another priest gets up from the chesterfield club chair and waits to be introduced; an uninspiring kind of fellow by the looks of him. A bit weedy and bookish, says the manly priest.

"This is Father Jeremy. He's very interested in your charts." He nods, no handshake. He looks about fifty, but it might be the grey hair, dark spectacles and mandatory sense of humour bypass as evidenced by the deep frown lines. No wonder numbers are down across the board, too many like him and not enough Robbie Coltranes.

"Father Jeremy, pleased to meet you." I nod back, poker face doing the bland. I hope it wasn't the unfriendly face, I can't always get them right.

"Let's sit gentlemen. Sherry?" Bishop Michael is the convivial host. I sit in the chair farthest from him, old habits die hard. Soon the tinkling decanter has filled a trio of glasses and we can begin. Sherry is a great start.

"The charts are most fascinating." The voice soft and smooth, escapes father Jeremy's lips. No fags or excessive booze in his past then. "They depict an alignment of stars that suggests adherence to a set of writings from the fifteen-eighties." He pauses. If he's expecting rational comment he's sorely disappointed. We're all agog and waiting. Is Santa Claus real?

"Vincenzo de Pedastalli, was an astronomer of the Left Hand Path and his writings talk of celestial sabbats that can open portals to places we are not meant to go." Oh fuck, this isn't good news. Bishop Michael has finished his sherry and so have I.

"His writings perished, allegedly, soon after his excoriation and recanting. It seems that the Vatican wanted them made safe for the future." Father Jeremy didn't quite let the sneer reach his lips, but there was a definite wrinkling of the nose. Was it due to shit that hit the fan four centuries ago and had percolated into a coming shit-storm? Probably.

"These star charts are modern, not ancient." I point out, helpful wee soul that I am. Best not have any misconceptions.

"Indeed, but they have been copied from a very credible source, showing one or two minor errors that existed on the original charts." Rolling out the charts Father Jeremy points to three transparent little post-its. I look up smartly.

"How do we know what was on the originals? Weren't they destroyed? Made safe?" I try not to let my incredulity fill my voice and fail. No wonder we are in the shit, regularly. Making things safe obviously does not mean what I think it means.

"One set of his works still exists in the Vatican Library vault. The originals were burned on the orders of, the then pope, Gregory the Thirteenth." Father Jeremy has been digging hard, it seems. We should all be thankful to Gregory the thirteenth.

"If one copy exists, why not another eh? Is that it?" The Bishop has caught on pretty quickly and he doesn't look happy and he's very slow to refill I notice. Maybe if I waggle my glass a little more?

"So our Friends have seen a copy. Or perhaps a copy of a copy of a copy. So?" My patience is wearing thin due to blood infiltrating my alcohol stream. My frown lines are deepening by the moment.

"There is a Celestial Sabbat soon, we think." Jeremy drops his bombshell and stops. Cue the dramatic music and ominous looks.

"Do these actually exist? Do they really open portals?" Lots of mumbo-jumbo gets written and because it's old some people believe it. Look at some of the stuff included in the Book, not exactly literal or credible at times.

"Perhaps. I have been tracing back through de Pedastalli's works and have discerned various dates on which an alignment may have taken place." He sipped his sherry before flipping open his notebook. His handwriting looks like chicken scratchings or hieroglyphics and is totally unintelligible upside down. I can usually read upside down writing. It has gotten me out of trouble regularly.

"Four times in the nineteenth century, three times in the twentieth and the next one is within five years, as near as I can tell. Of course it may already have occurred. Calculations of this type are notoriously difficult and unreliable." He concludes looking over reading glasses.

I love information like this. I try not to be sarcastic but it does tend to seep out. However, sometimes I don't actually try very hard and this was going to be one of them.

"Do the portal's actually open?" Which, after all, is the

important bit. At least I think it is the important bit.

"There is evidence to suggest they do. However, the portals let things in, they don't let mankind out." He raises his hand to stop me butting in, "The Summa Exorcisma lists events that roughly correspond to these Celestial Sabbat. It appears Vincenzo di Pedastalli was correct."

"Not exactly good news then. Within the next five years all hell breaks loose." I get in past the raised hand.

"Quite, Andrew, quite." Bishop Michael was reaching for the sherry. Personally, I think, scotch would be more appropriate. Sherry just doesn't cut it sometimes. He has noticed my empty glass though.

"How do they open these portals? A specific ritual? A location? A sacrifice?" I head to the land of the practical, after all I am on the ground and will probably be deployed to assist.

"We don't know." Father Jeremy's frown deepens, "There have been accounts of all of those. There is no clear pattern emerging from the histories."

"This might cause us a problem then. What if a whole bunch of Satanists decide to open portals all over the place? We'd be in trouble if it worked." The drama queen in me is getting out soon to be followed by the screaming panic merchant.

"Only one portal opens at a time, and only opened for the minute at midnight. According to Vincenzo, and he's been right about everything else."

"Well we've got to be thankful for that." Bishop Michael looking for the upside. An upside which I doubt, very much, there will be. His sherry has evaporated.

"So the portal is open for a minute and what happens to the visitor? Do they get pulled back or are they our guest until we send them on their way?" See a sensible contribution. However, I am self-interested, it'll be me or someone like me who'll have to do the sending. Happy bunny, I am not.

"It would stay until despatched." Father Jeremy looks smug, knowing he's not holding that bag. Bollocks.

Driving home to sunny Gleninch in the dark, and probably over the legal alcohol limit due to a few sherries and claret inside me, I start to replay the dinner conversation. It was all 'what if' and supposition, with the odd 'according to Vincenzo' thrown in for good measure. Father Jeremy wasn't nearly as dull as I had expected; his dry sense of humour appealed to me. My sense of the ridiculous didn't appear to sit too well with Bishop Michael. His loss.

I didn't share my recent run in with the local traffic cops nor did I share my latest lead on organ trafficking. Not sure why I didn't but it could wait. Besides if I had mentioned progress Michael would want it all wrapped up quickly. And I was no where near that yet.

It's funny how the mind starts to play tricks. After one hard knee in the nuts every pair of headlights coming up behind had me worrying if a second instalment was going to be delivered. Not fear, exactly, more trepidation. It was interrupting my Sherlock Holmes routine. I just wanted to be back in my room with the door locked (after checking for hexes). I had a few nagging questions. Organ smuggling, how does that work? And how did the bad guys kill MacPhail? I should probably add why to that list too. The answers I had were all beginning to sound the same; I have no fucking idea.

What a rigmarole, keeping my room door open with one foot while checking for hexes on the inside handle. Just because they have done me once already doesn't mean they won't do it again. No hexes that I can see or feel, so I step in and let the door close with a click. Paranoia has set in, flicking the lights on I check the shower curtain for a Norman Bates-a-gram. The room is safe, apparently. As untidy as I left it; no tidy up elves here then. I smile to myself, more in relief than anything else, and pour myself a large one. It helps me sleep. Drunken stupors do that, you know.

The smile, incongruous at best on my face, slides off as I see an A4 manilla envelope lying on my pillow. The fucking fairies have been in again. Not impressed is an understatement, pissed off is much, much closer.

"Secure room, what a fucking joke." I snarl as I snatch up the envelope. Fuck the evidence trail, there won't be a fingerprint anywhere on it. They are too bloody careful for that.

Where I was expecting a composite newspaper letter message, I am surprised to find some sort of shipping manifest and other documentation. Obviously someone wants to help me. A text would have been fine. My anger dissipates leaving a ridiculous look on my face, which I have just seen in the mirror. I am puzzled. These documents are trying to tell me something but I can't actually discern what exactly. It looks like it might be important though.

Chapter 17

The following morning as I collected the mail, from the 'knocking shop' as I had taken to calling MacPhail's old house, the phone rang. I considered ignoring it but, call me weak, but once I hear a phone ringing I need to answer it. After all it might be God eh? Anyway, the point is, it was ringing and I picked it up. I was totally unprepared for what happened next.

"Hello" I can answer the phone like an adult, sometimes. The delay, you know the empty pause, told me it was an overseas call, quite a way overseas, if the reception was anything to go by. Who would be phoning a dead priest? I started thinking about how to break the news. I'm not great at this sort of thing.

"Father MacPhail, please." Accent was a bit British but not quite. The caller was about to get some bad news. I drew a breath and tried my solemn voice.

"I'm afraid, Father MacPhail is no longer here." I began, best priest voice. I didn't want to just blurt out 'He's dead', although given his practices I maybe could get away with it.

"Give him a message for me yeah? The container has cleared customs in Johannesburg without any problems. Got it yeah?" It was a South African accent. What effing container? A container of what?

"Who will I say called?" Pumping time. Any info would be a help.

"Den Beer, Marc Den Beer, got that yeah? Den Beer." The reception was so poor, he could have been saying Mars bar. I didn't let on that I wasn't sure of his words.

"I've got it thanks. I'll let him know the container has passed customs. OK. Bye." Best to keep it simple, lessens chance of giving myself away. I put the receiver down and let out the breath that I'd been holding. This tied in nicely with my clue present from the other night. If only I could pull them together. Serendipity, that's what it is. A chance happening that gave me a clue. And like all usual clues, I had no idea what the hell to do with it. There's a funny thing about clues. They seem to be like buses, never there when you want one then two or three turn up at once.

This case was beginning to make my head hurt. Permanently. I had been here three weeks and had made next to no progress. At least now I had a workable hypothesis. Murderer? No idea, something supernatural certainly. Victim? Bad, bad man who had more sex than anyone had a right to. A cult in the congregation? Yep, but no idea who they were and how they operated. A sorcerer, who knows what he's doing making the whole thing very dangerous. I was totally screwed. Now this clue may indeed be a fresh impetus to my bumbling. I would be guarding it like a squirrel hoards nuts.

South Bloody Africa, a new focus on MacPhail's extra clerical activities was most definitely called for. I suppose I'd best go back to square one, a place I know well, and look for African clues. The manse was littered with artefacts after all.

"Brotherton, How are you?" Start off normal, it helps you know, breaks the ice. Probably a good idea to build up to my great unveiling of a combination of clues.

"Good thanks. You?" That's my boy, no clues to those around him. Secret squirrel eat your heart out. Next we would be having a secret handshake or password.

"Good. I need 5 minutes with you, today if you can manage it." Keeping to the point and allowing him the opportunity to say very little in public,.

"Great idea, say 6pm at yours?" By mine he means the hotel that I had been incarcerated in. It was functional and anonymous and perfect for a clandestine-in-plain-view-drop.

"No probs, I'll see you in the bar." A priest in a bar, a cliche if ever there was one. Not that we all have a drink problem you understand. It was public but fine for a handover of information. I plan to give him my thoughts on the organ trail and the call from

Den Beer that morning. He would be best placed to pull out a narrative that we could explore and pursue.

His professional detective skills would be needed to bring down the ring. My skills would be needed to deal with the dabblers and their master. Bishop Michael would be needed to hush it all up afterwards. What a team eh? Practically the X-Men. So what did I actually have? A phone call, a manifest and a 'black liver' comment from an old racist. What did I not have? Any real idea how it all hangs together or who the hell was hanging it all together.

It's a pretty poor excuse for a bar but at least it has tables and sells food. Okay, I admit it, I am a snob at times. The food is limited to something and chips or chicken tikka ding. However, I won't starve and the beer is not too bad. The padded stools and red velour booths have seen better days and no doubt conform to the contours of some regular's arse. I am a little fidgety as I await Brotherton. My large manilla envelope gets moved around and fondled like the Precious. If I start saying 'Gollum' I will be beyond any chance of recovery. I swig the remnants of my first pint; it didn't last long. I am about to get a refill when Inspector Brotherton makes an appearance. He gets the refills, good man. Thirsty work this detective thing.

"I know what's going on!" I blurt out, all pretence of being cool, discrete and secretive gone. No one in the bar seems to have noticed my outburst. Which is probably just as well.

"Keep it down, man." Brotherton remembered where we were. I had been bouncing about all day, excited at my breakthrough and needing someone to tell. For a man who can hear secrets and keep them under the seal of the sacrament of the confession, I should be able to manage you'd think. Apparently not.

"Sorry. It's true though." I slide the manilla envelope across the damp copper topped table. Evidence now in the hands of the authorities, as it were. I have copies just in case. I lean forward, all secret-service like, careful not to knock over my pint.

"It's all about organ trafficking. MacPhail is just part of the chain; stretching from here to South Africa and beyond. In that envelope is the start of the proof, the smoking gun." I'm too earnest when I am excited, and Brotherton is edging away, trying to escape the crazy man.

"Proof? In here? But why did they kill MacPhail then?" Pockets asks the bit I don't bloody know. Bloody police training. I slump like a burst balloon that has had its air seep out. I reach for the pint of reviving lager.

"I don't know that bit but he was in it up to his neck. I had a call from South Africa telling me the container had passed customs with no problems." As if that proved my point. It does sort of. Well, it helps at any rate.

"That doesn't prove anything, though." Brotherton raises his hand to stop me interrupting, which I was about to do. "But it does suggest a course of enquiry. We'll need to be careful not to spook the horses. If we do they'll close up shop and move on to somewhere else." Brotherton swigs his pint, the foamy moustache disappears quickly as he wipes with the back of his hand.

Time to play my trump card. "I had an interesting visit to a member of my congregation in hospital the other day. He let slip that he'd paid for a liver and he didn't want a black one." I smile, see told you. Letting the narrative build one piece at a time.

"Well, we have a link to follow. What's his name?" Brotherton seems more interested now. He has a tangible witness and accomplice with reach and a line of enquiry. I expect to see a happy cop face, soon.

"All in the envelope." What a pro I am, prepared and everything. "He's also in their little cult, so I'll be pursuing my own enquiries on that front."

"Be careful then. And keep me posted. There's big money in organ trafficking. They've murdered one priest, I doubt they'd baulk at making that two." Mr Doom and Gloom strikes again and no sign of happy cop.

"I'll be careful." Thanks mate, thanks a lot.

Chapter 18

Evening Prayer was always my favourite service; it set me at peace as a teenager each night before going home to a somewhat chaotic home life. My father having left years before and mum's boyfriend, well least said about that the better. The beautiful simplicity of the words, even now, brings me calm. When I was a teenager at evening prayer, it was often just me and the priest. I bet he thought I was a strange kid but he was always kind to me. A real man of God; dead now, of course.

I needed some peace tonight. This morning news came through, on the BBC no less, that the Gleninch Priest Killer had hanged himself in his cell, whilst on remand. A note was left on the floor and he was found hanging. Piss dripping off his shoes, eyes bulging and mouth agape he wasn't a pretty sight apparently. Didn't get that on the news. Of course with his demise they thought I would, no doubt, be recalled from Gleninch. It was over, or at least it was meant to be. A fit of swearing had taken over my usual grumpiness and it wasn't helped when Brotherton dropped by after mid morning to fill me in on the details.

"The note looks iffy to me." He started with the obvious.

My peevishness was writ large on my face, so he soldiered on. "He was barely bloody literate when I took his confession and now his suicide note reads like Dan-bloody-Brown." Way to go, Brotherton. He is beginning to sound like me. Imitation being the highest form of flattery.

"Of course, there'll be no investigation. Open and shut case. They want this to go away." He concluded, didn't even use his notebook. He was as frustrated as I was, apparently. My disgust at this turn of events was obvious and normally my responses would be calm, measured, erudite even.

"Fucking Bastards." Was the best I could manage. I stomped into the Vestry to get out of my outfit. Inspector Brotherton followed me in and shut the door quietly. I was still growling under my breath as he waited. The staccato nature of my movements adding a level of violence to my anger culminating in a tear of my cassock. I manage to grind my teeth rather than let out another high volume expletive.

"The shipping note you gave me was for a consignment of organ transplant boxes." He was speaking quietly forcing me to stop stomping about. Making me stop and listen, once the purple chasuble was over my head.

"And?"

"They were for onward shipping through a few different import-export companies until they ended up in Kenya, a little town called Lamooro." He paused again to see if I was keeping up. I was.

"MacPhail's little friends in Africa. Why would they need a whole container of organ transplant boxes? A few maybe, but a container load?" I was folding my vestments, badly, and trying to stow them neatly. A task that seemed beyond me at that moment.

"Exactly, they wouldn't." Brotherton knew in his gut we were on to something. I just wasn't quite there yet. The dates on the manifest were way before the Den Beer call and didn't match up with the clearing customs comment.

"So what the fuck do they do with them then?" I knew that expletives were building up in direct proportion with my lack of understanding. My mother always said it was a weakness of vocabulary to swear so much, I was such a disappointment.

"There's been a civil war in neighbouring Mozambique or Somalia. I think they are harvesting them there. There's very little control in that whole region. It's like the bloody wild west." No notebook for this either. We were well and truly off the record. I wondered what he had done with my evidence.

"And then they sell them all over the world? That's a heck of a big job. Wouldn't someone notice?" I like a good conspiracy theory but this would be huge. And all from a casual statement from a racist bigot. Ain't Karma a bitch.

"Proof, that's the problem. We haven't got any." Inspector

Rain-on-the-parade stated making sure I wasn't getting ahead of myself.

"I have that problem regularly. This organ traffic is funding a satanic organisation and its many contacts, and you want proof. Do you think MacPhail was about to blow the whistle?" My musing out loud often helps if someone else is listening and can make some semblance of sense of it all. I look at him, perhaps a little too expectantly.

"It gives us a motive. Still we need to work this further. I have a forensic accountant working on the flows of the money; hopefully that will turn up something." The old team back together, but this time Brotherton couldn't afford to get caught.

"So the MacPhail murder case is closed then. No one will be looking any further. What did you do with the manifest?" I sounded disappointed even to me but I needed to know in case Brotherton was ever removed.

"That ship has sailed but let's see what else we can do. They got Capone for tax evasion after all. The manifest is filed in the shoplifting file for David Graham, only we know it is there. A classic misfiling." Inspector Brotherton the optimist. Me? I'd stick to complaining about the unfairness of it all.

Chapter 19

It is probably not a good idea to tell the nice policeman that the reason I want access to MacPhail's manse is to perform a working. You know, magic. They might take a dim view of it after all. I used the 'I need to gather some congregation details that Father MacPhail has in his (that is our) manse. It worked so much better after all. No tricky questions just a simple smile and nod of assent. A well mannered policeman keeping watch over my back should have been reassuring but after my traffic cop meeting I was somewhat wary. I locked the door from the inside, quietly.

So anyway, I wanted to remove and disperse some of the power of Darkness that still resonated from the house. Well, in particular, from the circle on the living room floor. It had been etched many times and as such held a deep rooted nexus, the darkness of the enemy. Just sitting in his armchair had brought tears and pain to me, so God knows what rolling back his circle would be like. A picnic in the sunshine it would not be.

After turning the key in the lock and locking out the rest of the world, I stepped forward to a place I'd rather not go. The sun, however, bolstered my spirits. I wouldn't want to be doing this after dark. It was almost noon, so I had plenty of time to complete the working and be on my way before Dark-rise. Or True Dark if you prefer.

Funny how unoccupied buildings have a smell. Not a damp musty smell but simply a smell; as if to say 'this is not a place of the living'. How very appropriate for this place. MacPhail was certainly gone but his vibrations could still be felt, or at least I could still feel them. I left the key in the lock. The door was secured; no one would be interrupting me. The last thing I needed was someone to walk in mid-incantation as it were.

"I come to cleanse this place with the Host of our Lord. In the name of the Father, The Son and the Holy spirit." My voice full of authority. No explosion or supernatural phenomena in response, so I began the Walk. The Walk. The steps of Our Lord Jesus Christ along the streets of Jerusalem, around him enemies, scorn and hatred. In this place I could feel the air tight with anticipation. The sun was high in the sky, this is my time.

"I hear your taunts, your jeers, your curses but the blood of My Lord was spilled to redeem me. His steps, filled with pain, cleanse these stones as once they trod the paths of Jerusalem." I stepped up each step making the sign of the cross, bringing the blessing of the Lord to each space in the house. It took less than an hour. I did think the bedroom might need special attention as the whiff of corruption seemed to have seeped into the very fabric of the building. I cast open the windows and scattered the essence that pervaded the bedroom. Like the casting down of the money lenders in the temple, the throwing open my arms scattered the sexual residue of magic built up by the many sessions of MacPhail.

I walked every room except the living room where the circle was etched. The knocking shop that was the bedroom, the main event so far. When I reached the front door again I took a moment to open my spirit. This was always a bit hit or miss, any residual trouble might strike now.

I walked each room again 'open' to the psychic or supernatural forces that may have been present. I sought out the little pockets of the Dark that could have been missed as I walked before. If I had started this way I would have been swamped and overwhelmed by the darkness and pain that had been present. The blessing and the walk of Our Lord had washed away the malignant residue of MacPhail and his cronies. This house felt a much more wholesome place, with only a passing memory of the darkness that had filled it.

I felt a darkness at the edge of my vision, as I passed the meter cupboard. I had not opened this space and had missed a possible hiding place. It was a strong sink of Darkness, being probably the darkest spot in the whole house. I blessed myself and the door before tugging the handle. Inside, beside the Vacuum cleaner and the dusters, blackness seeped from the floor. No carpet covering the floor, I could see the dark sigils of power warding against me. A magical booby trap on a floorboard, what lay beneath I had no idea but it worried me that someone had felt the need to ward against the powers of light. I wondered, which is like hesitation or dithering but much more meaningful. I finally decided. I would trust my protection and I pulled it up. Good eh?

When I have the host in my pocket and unction on my forehead, I feel bullet-proof. Experience would suggest otherwise as often I have been caught out a bit. The jolt that fired up my arm was strong and left me lying half upright against the opposite wall. A stunned moment passed as I caught up. Breath rasping as I sucked it back into my lungs.

"Bastard." A single swearword to encapsulate my feelings. The dark sigils remained intact, although invisible to the human eye. They had acted like a sharp rebuke, and a casual reminder that these were no fools. Why this had been missed when they had cleared out the evidence? Had MacPhail been keeping secrets from his own side? I would be finding out soon. The sigils emanating a 'nothing to see here' may have kept the untrained eyes away.

A prayer of cleansing and the sprinkling of Holy water should render the sigils powerless this time. I reached out and pulled up the floorboard. The Hammer house of horror creak that accompanied my pulling was startlingly loud in the confined space. There in the space below was a black velvet puddle. Inside the velvet was something vaguely rectangular, I presumed so anyway. I squatted there and looked into the secret hiding place. I opened my spirit to feel around the edges. I felt a depth to this darkness far further than the foot or so it seems in the physical world. Deep inside this little place was a pit of pure darkness, a well into the Otherworld. Which came first? The well or the manse? Or was this manse deliberately sited here because of the well? If that were the case then every single Priest in this parish had been of the enemy and the fingers of Evil had spread widely indeed.

A horrible thought struck me. I looked round as the worry began to build in my imagination. If the Manse was specifically put here what of the church itself? What about it? Was it compromised and unsanctified? Desecrated? It didn't feel that way but then again I hadn't been looking for that.

"In the name of Our Lord Jesus Christ, and of Saint Michael and his Angels, I abjure your Evil. Feel the cleansing power of Our Lord in the purity of this Holy Water and let it wash away the Evil contained within. Blessed is he that comes in the Name of the Lord, Hosanna in the highest." I put forth my hand and sprinkle more holy water before pulling forth the velvet package.

It is heavy and feels almost as if someone is holding it and trying to pull it back in. With a wrench I pull it free. From the velvet material power ripples across my hands like a static charge or pins and needles. I move back into the sunlight carrying it before me. The kitchen is closest and filled with sunshine.

I dump the package on the kitchen island and flick open the velvet wrap. A book was protected within the folds of, very expensive and old, velvet. The air is still but inside my mind I hear the hissing of the sunlight as it caresses and cleanses this evil artefact. The leather is old and well worn. The red, almost a burgundy, leather is etched and tooled with a fleur-de-lys edging. In the centre a tiger's eye stone sits in a well and around the whole a leather tie passes on three loops. It is sizzling still as the power contained within resists the sunlight and the power of light.

"Fuck." I manage to gasp as I stare at the shadows running over the surface. This is a major Arcana. I don't know what I should do with it. I want to open it but I know that is hazardous. I really should leave it alone and call in for some support but I am the Johnny on the spot. I drip some holy water onto the leather tie and then after blessing myself I slip the leather tie off and pull it free. My hands shake a little as I avoid contact with the book itself, although I know I will open it in a moment or two. I wet my lips and give a little cough, readying my voice should it be needed. I flip the page.

Inside on an ancient creamy page a pictorial representation of the satanic Goat covers the first page. The baleful scowl as it looks up at me, not quite so terrifying as I expected. The tingling in my finger tips is fading away. I turn the page gently, and realise I am holding onto a breath. I let it escape my lips slowly. I scan the next page, covered in dire warnings of disaster for all who have no right to look upon these words. My usual joviality has evaporated and this book has my fullest concentration. Outside, in the real world, the sun marches on across the sky.

The book is written in what looks like Latin, but there is something slightly off with some of the spelling. I can't really translate it, and shouldn't get too interested in trying to do so. I will pass this back to Bishop Michael and he can get it to the right place. This is a dangerous tome and needs to be studied and locked away. It appears to be the scripture and order of service for the worship of their Dark Satanic master. I close it and bind it shut. I am weary and my eyes feel gritty, somewhat like the morning after the night before. I sprinkle more Holy water and offer a benediction to ward and contain the dark words and evil intent contained inside. I have a working to do on the living room. The sun is slanting in now as the afternoon has passed in a blink. Fuck.

Leaving the tome in the kitchen and warding shut the door

under the stairs, I need to hurry or it will be dark before I am done. I announce my presence and push open the door. I am Daniel and I enter the mouth of the beast. I speak the words of our faith in Latin and then in English as I cross the threshold. I fear not as the Lord is with me. I am a tool in his hands.

"Begone, in the Name of the Father, Son and Holy Spirit. I command thee in his name.'" I step to the heavy drapes and throw them back. Sunlight floods in but a full third of the room is not touched directly. If only I had left the book until later.

I look around the room, my spirit eyes scanning and seeing the blood circle on the floor. It is deepest of black from the many old rituals performed here. I walk my way to the tip of his left horn and begin the walking back. Anti clockwise each step is a challenge to my authority. I feel the resistance like a thickening in the air. I can feel the hurt, the pain, the sex, the abuse and most of all in this room of tears I can taste the salt and hear the cries of anguish.

"Wash clean this dirt of sin, as our Lord washed the feet of the sinners. My service, oh Lord, is yours let these memories be washed away and cleansed from this place." I walk round and am at the horns again. This path has been worked many times. Not just by MacPhail but by his predecessors. The circle is strong and is resisting still. The power laid down time after time.

"I walk the many steps to Golgotha, let me carry the burden

of these sins as you once did, oh Lord. Let me be the unworthy vessel to break these bonds of evil." I passed round once more. I feel the evil tendrils gripping and tugging at my feet as I pass. They are powerless to prevent me but still they resist. In the shadows I feel a malevolence gathering, and its eyes bore into my back as I pass round time and again. Impotent and angry I can sense its frustration. The afternoon sun is running away and soon the circle and pentagram will be out of the direct rays. Things may get a bit interesting then.

The walking back of such a strong and well used pentagram was always going to take a while and I can feel the progress as the power seems to be fading at each turn. I am hopeful that I can complete the ritual before nightfall. The afternoon sun still strong is no longer on the floor and almost imperceptibly the mood in the room starts to change. I walk back another turn and am startled as I hear the cries of pain that once filled this room, echoes of a torment in the past. Memories of pain and tears, of hurt and torment, flood over me. Heart rending sobs burst from me. I am sharing their fates. I walk round again, more of a stumble as my eyes stream with tears. Tears that were shed years ago are relived by me as I pull myself around and around in the gathering gloom.

The feeble overhead light casts a dull yellow glow in the room as the sun has long since disappeared from the inside. The dark garden hedge casting a shadow over the garden shows the passing of time and the nearing of night. I am wrung out, as my emotions are shredded again and again. I know that each one I feel is set free forever, it is my pain to bear and just an echo of a great wrong.

I am shuffling now, and a new feeling begins. I can feel the change in the air. Lust. Before this room was filled with tears this circle was imbued with blood and sex magic. I lift my eyes and see flashes of another priest in MacPhail's chair with a succession of partners fellating, fucking, and masturbating in a frenzy of flickering images. My senses are overwhelmed and my body responds to these memories. I feel like a total slut in moments as I am at once one and many sexual servants to this man. My mouth recalls his taste, my body feels his penetration, the desires and releases flood me as I spurt and spurt incapable of resisting. I am spent as I complete this circle. A mocking laughter fills the room. I need to get out of here, like Douglas MacArthur 'I shall return.'

Outside, with the door closed behind me I try to catch my breath. I am gasping like a landed fish. Looking down to my groin the mess of my trousers is evident and feels totally icky.

"Fucks sake." I manage to walk like John Wayne to the kitchen and snatch up the now, hopefully, inert book and velvet. Sunlight is a hell of a thing.

Chapter 20

Outside of Gleninch there's an old tower, monument thing. Well, actually, it's on the other side of the Lomond Hills which are sometimes called the Paps of Fife. Although to be blunt, they are the most misshapen pair of boobs on the planet and if you include Largo Law then there are three of them. Go figure.

Anyway, a message to meet my reluctant informer at a remote monument was just too irresistible for me. So I had set off at lunchtime in my happy, little 'here I am' red car and was almost there when a chained forestry commission gate barred my way. I thought, wrongly, that there was a road all the way and no outside walking would be needed. Pulled up short in a tight pine forest (plantation not a real forest) and feeling hemmed in, I have to reverse up the road to a wide bit. It's all relative but there appear to be something like passing places along the track. Ahead of me, beyond the gate, a hard core track of mud and grey aggregate leads onwards and upwards to the monument. The gate must be new-ish as I have walked here a few times when youthful exuberance made me tramp over the local hills. I didn't remember this track nor the gate.

I looked down at my footwear and held out little hope that I could pick my way through without falling on my arse. As for the gate, I hoped not to fall off as I swung my legs over. Ordinarily I would have walked round but the quagmire to the sides looked like a disaster waiting to happen. It would be bad enough with mud covering my shoes and new trouser hem, the older pair didn't survive the vomit coating, but I didn't want to meet my informant plastered in grey mud from arsehole to elbow.

I was almost half a mile from it, clouds overhead didn't look that bad, so I left the brolly and pulled up my collar. Ah the country. Why is it always bloody freezing? Perhaps that is a question that is only asked in northern climes. Even in the summer it isn't actually hot, I personally would settle for warm occasionally. Now I know traipsing off into the wilds is like a trap from a horror movie. I can almost hear myself snorting at the screen. I am not that stupid. I've left a note for Brotherton and I have a few weapons with me. Holy water, unction, Magnum 357- probably the most powerful handgun in the world (not the last one). I also have a slick torch that I bought, with batteries, at the garage this morning. I've even tested it, maglite apparently, LED and bright as hell. So I'm all prepared, obviously.

Black leather Gibson shoes are so not for tramping along forestry roads, as my slipping and stumbling attests to. The mud is all over them and lines the bottoms of my trousers; it's a brown-grey clingy, clumpy mud that will be an utter pig to get out. Anyway, I tramp along with indelicate language spilling from my lips. At least no-one can hear me. Or at least I hope no one can.

Some minutes of tip-toeing and swearing later, I break through the trees as the tended grass of the monument comes into view. On my right a large stone tower, with a cracking view out over the Howe of Fife, looms up above me. A view that is well worth the walk if not the mud. Farms and fields sweeping away to the mountains in the distance and the wind cutting through my clothes. Bracing, I believe, it's called. Apparently my clothes are totally unsuitable and offer next to no protection from the wind at all. Wind Chill factor; if it gets any colder my tonsils will have company.

Is this a wild goose chase or a trap? I have a quick recce round the tower with a casual look inside the open doorway, while trying not to look like a pratt. I now know that it was erected in honour of Onesipherious Tyndall- Bruce in 1855, and is called the Tyndall Bruce monument, so not a wasted trip then. There is no one inside, I checked with my new torch, but it was very dark. I am suspicious by nature and am beginning to feel set up. Checking my phone I discover that it is a zero bar zone and no phoning for help will be happening anytime soon. Stooging around the monument, I feel exposed. My early bravado at agreeing to meet here has evaporated to be replaced by a nagging ache in the pit of my stomach. Not quite fear but might build into it given time.

On about my third lap, I notice something blue at the foot of the viewpoint. Well, on the ground below the rail to be precise, it looks like a rain jacket. Funny how the human brain refuses to recognise some things, broken bloody bodies at the foot of a large drop being one of them. I was staring for, what seemed to me at any rate, ages until it dawned on me. This might be my anonymous ally. Bloody hell of a coincidence that the site of my secret rendezvous, should come with a body.

Slowly, my brain started to work and I whirled round away from the rail fence. Don't want a helping hand, as it were. I can feel the shaking begin as I fumble for my phone. Shock makes the brain slow and body problematic. I can't get my pocket zip open. I'm pulling and tugging and finally it gives up spilling forth its contents. Luckily the ground is soft and springy which prevents it smashing to smithereens. I am clumsy enough without shock and you'd think I was picking up a bar of soap as it takes three goes to get it into my hand. Using both hands I manage to steady the screen enough to realise there is no signal.

"Fuck!" fear is setting in. Will I be helped over the edge too? I can feel the saliva gathering in my mouth. For god's sake I am going to hurl. I spit and spit, trying to stave it off but soon the heaving starts and my cookies are well and truly tossed. I am an easy target. If they wanted me out of the frame, now it would be easy to facilitate it. I decide to leg it. A stumbling, stagger of a run but with my footwear it soon turns into a knee scraping, muddy fall down and stagger up kind of thing. I am covered from almost head to toe. I am a mess. A terrified, soggy muddy mess.

Obviously my description, garbled as it was, is sufficient. Before long two police cars and an ambulance have filled the road behind my car. The gate is in the process of being unchained. Some constable has my keys and is behind the wheel of my Nissan. I have recovered some coherence. Now I just look a state. Where is Brotherton? I don't trust any of this mob, I am surrounded in the countryside but the ball kicker isn't among them. A nice young sergeant is trying to get me to sit in his car, in the back I notice. I sit on the bonnet, all cold and shivery. I'm sure he is waiting on an answer. He asked something a moment ago. No idea what it was though?

"Father, are you all right?" He uses his best solicitous tone. He probably thinks it helps. It doesn't, by the way.

"Do you know the person who was killed?" Pushing, hard but not too hard. He may have been asking that for a while but I wasn't really with it.

"Yes, well actually no I don't." I manage to blab. Bollocks. No was the answer. Shock making dissembling difficult either that or the cold and mud.

"Which is it? Yes or no?" His patience has evaporated, and he now starts looking less than certain of my role in the event. I can see he isn't sure that my hands didn't do the helping.

"I don't." Better and firmer this time. I'd probably best not mention my rendezvous. Otherwise a whole new line of difficult questions might start to need answering. A bit like Pandora's box, once it is opened the trouble starts.

"What brought you out here, father?" His suspicious mind is working overtime. Hardly surprising. What are the chances of someone falling to their death in a remote place to be discovered before they are cold?

"The view." I am a bit surly and it doesn't sit well with the nice policeman. He has obviously had the sense of humour bypass that all uniformed officers get at the Police training college. He gives me the look, one from which I am immune. I look blandly back. He waits. He isn't sure if he wants to get in trouble for detaining the witness or for letting the killer escape.

A sigh escapes him, recognising that I am not saying anything else. His radio bleeps into life and a 'Two-six receiving' is swiftly spoken as he turns away. I can hear every word but I am not surprised when words like accident and instantaneous are decipherable. Perhaps I won't have to flash my card after all. I wonder if I will need Brotherton as a character witness. It might be better to leave him out of it, for now. Protect his pension for a little longer. His shoulders seem to slump as more information is relayed. Obviously I will be going soon; he has no need to keep me here. You never know, he might want to interview me anyway. Such is my sparkling line in wit and repartee. Perhaps the lamp in the eyes and wring a confession from me is on the menu.

"Father Steel," he turns round slowly, obviously having come to a decision. 'Can you come down to the station and give a statement?' He manages to make it sound optional.

"Now or later?" I decide that he'll have to work. Never get into a car with a strange man I was always told. Policemen count as strange men.

"Now would be best. Get it done and let you get on your way." Ooh a fencer. I bet he's just going to want a full search and check under the nails of the body. Stalling for time and trying to keep his options open.

"Sergeant, I want to go home and change my clothes. I can give you a statement here and now if that will suffice?" See, me the height of reasonableness. I am bloody freezing and have had just about enough of this nonsense. My inner child might escape and a tantrum ensue.

Before he can answer, the radio interrupts again. He's walking away a bit. I see a smile playing on his lips. I bet he can see a promotion coming as he makes a collar on a murder. Purposefully he walks over to me, a new spring in his step, a grim little smile on his face. His cuffs come out as he slaps one on my wrist. The steel colder than I am.

"I am detaining you on suspicion of murder." He turns me round and cuffs my wrists together. He's doing the blah, blah, blah that he needs to do. He isn't very gentle either, his excitement getting the better of him.

"Do you have anything to say?" He pauses. I snort derisively but he thinks he's Taggart, with a dodgy Fife accent, obviously. We are going to get along famously, I imagine. At least he ducks my head as he puts me in the back of his nice car. Oh well its going to be one of those days. I wonder if I'll get a cup of tea. Maybe a couple of digestives?

Chapter 21

I am being, what is called by the police, 'processed'. I wonder at which point I should whip out my get-out-of-jail-free-card. The smug bastard with the cuffs is going to be disappointed. I look forward to that moment, you know the 'get it right up ye' moment. However, at the moment I am looking at the messy state of my clothes. I think there is a mud free bit somewhere. They are getting a bit uncomfortable as they stick to me and the hard plastic chair I have to sit on. I suppose it could be worse, no full body search yet. No hosing down or rubber hose treatment. I wonder if these things ever really did happen. No tea yet either.

The door opens and two plain clothed chaps wander in. I wonder if they are from the same mould as the arresting officer. I suppose I am about to find out. I compose my face in the blandest look I can manage. But I really struggle as I can still smell and taste my own vomit from earlier. It just makes me look like a sour puss. I hope they can smell it, too.

One presses down the record buttons on the two cassette recorder. His spotty cheeks a hangover from his unwashed youth and the sneer well practised in front of the mirror in the mornings.

He tries to glare at me but I am distracted by the burgeoning carbuncle on the side of his nose and the creamy pus beginning to present itself. The tone denotes the race has started. Time and date stamps are blathered at the machine as well as the names of those present. He looks at me, all stern and serious, he's seen Taggart too,

"Father Steel?" Starts Tweedledum. They join me at the table, a manilla folder in front of them with lots of contents. Photos, I expect. Lurid and close up of the impact of a rapid descent onto rocks. I guess I'd better confess quick.

"I am Detective Sergeant McKay, this is Detective Constable Davidson." He nods at his partner. So they aren't called Tweedledum and Tweedledumber? Shocking. I don't offer anything, just let him go on. Why interrupt his preprepared speech? Wouldn't want to throw him off into a series of ehm's and ehs.

"I am going to question you, before I do so I must caution you, you are not obliged to answer any of these questions but any answers you give will be noted and may be used in evidence against you." The preliminaries are over. Worst foreplay ever.

"Do you know why you are being detained?" He pauses, waiting for me. I suppose I'd better take part in this farce. I sigh, heavily, and regret it smelling again the vomit from earlier.

"I am being detained because your officer on the scene has a very vivid imagination and the inability to think past Taggart.' I didn't mean that to come out, oh well. Here we go. There won't be tea anytime soon after that.

"You are a murder suspect chummy, so cut that lip or you'll regret it." DC Tweedledumber barks out. Ooh he is so terrifying. I smile, a smug 'Fuck off Spotty' if ever I saw one. I should stop pissing about but I am now entrenched and not letting this pass easily.

"You must belong to the same school of pointless police training I suppose." I love the colour that flushes his face. It might be called puce.

"Murder is a very serious matter Father Steel. I suggest you answer the questions properly." Much better, DS Tweedledumb is quite calm.

"Why did you shove him over the rail?" dumber leans forward, all attempted menace. Comical stuff really.

"I didn't." I snort, and instantly wish I hadn't. That little moment of having to swallow down the remnants of back-of-the-nose sickness and trying not to heave again was upon me. I hung in there, just.

"Why were you out there?" DS Dumb, tries from his side. "His number was on your phone?" Really, I wonder about that. It said withheld when the call came in.

"Sight seeing." I might as well have said 'fuck off'. His

gambit had failed. I moved in my seat eliciting a squelching noise from the muddy trousers sticking to the plastic.

"Father, this is serious and you are in the frame for murder." He pulls out a picture of one of my parishioners, all broken and bloody. It is the still from first arrival at the scene. Pretty Gruesome. "Tell me what happened, it will save us all a great deal of time." Aww bless he is trying to coax me into blabbing.

"Who is this?" DS Dumber blurts from his side. He really needs to re-attend basic training and learn the art of shutting up.

"Colin somebody, Patterson I think." I can be helpful. He lives alone though so unless they are going to inform his cat, I can't point them anywhere else. Anyway it clears up who was helping me.

"So you knew each other then." I missed which one of them uttered the words as I looked at the wreckage of a decent man lying before me in glorious colour. It saddened me that he had been killed for trying to help me solve the mess. Another victim of the MacPhail gang. Retribution would find them, all of them. My face took on a stony look which the illustrious detectives took to mean something.

"He is one of the congregation of St Margaret's in the Fields, in Gleninch." I try hard to keep my voice even. I can feel the anger churning inside me.

"So why were you out there together then?" DC Dumber,

again.

"We weren't together." I have just about had enough of these clowns. Will I ask for Brotherton or pull out my God Squad ID? Decisions, decisions.

"Pretty fishy both being there at the same time. Middle of nowhere. Stinks Father, totally stinks. Why did you kill him?" DC Dumber continues. He would be out of his depth in a puddle. I look at him, like the thick shit he is.

"Pfft." I make a noise but not a snort after last time. I have learned that lesson the hard way.

"A lovers tryst gone wrong?" He soldiers on obviously unaware of the old adage 'better to remain silent and look a fool than to speak and remove all doubt'.

"You may fancy him but he's not my type." My smart mouth designed to get me in to bother. DC homophobe jumps to his feet, all flushed and angry. Go on, I dare you my face screams at him. My arrogance designed to elicit a response. His boss gets him in check with a look. Good doggie, sit. He has decided something.

"We are formally detaining you and will need DNA samples and your clothes for analysis. Perhaps afterwards you'll be prepared to cooperate." DS Dumb, flaps the folder shut. He doesn't look happy.

Fuck them, let them waste their time. Not surprised so many

crimes are unsolved. This lot couldn't find their arse with both hands and a team of sniffer dogs. More processing then. Still no tea.

After a brief interlude in the stupidity a uniformed officer comes in with a paper onesie for me and a big poly bag for my clothes. It will be a pleasure to get the muddy mess off and be in a nice clean outfit. White is so fattening, I look like I have gained three stone since Christmas. Never mind, I am sure I can get back to my fighting weight for the Olympics. Not very likely though.

"Press that buzzer when you are changed Father." What a polite young fellow, He leaves me to the task in hand. So I spare him some of the more acidic responses in my repertoire. He is just getting on with his job.

"I will. Thank you. Any chance of tea?" If you don't ask, as they say. He smiles, maybe he has heard about the interview.

"I will see what I can do. NATO standard?" He seems utterly lacking in hostility. Milk and two is fine and I nod, although hot and wet would do. Stripping off muddy, vomit encrusted clothes is a task for celebrity jungle programmes, not one I had really wanted to try out personally. Vomit splatter is bad enough but the heavy clumpy sticky mud has stuck my hairy legs to the inside of my trousers and is worse than a band aid being pulled off. I am wincing like a woose as I get myself disentangled. Fun it is not. Anyway, the buzzer is well and truly pressed.

A few minutes, spanning an eternity, pass and a mug of tea arrives as my bag of mud-cakes is taken away for processing. I only get a sip when DS Dumb (or dumber) arrives in a somewhat unhappy mood. He slaps my wallet on the table. He has run a check on my ID. Oh dear, the disappointment must be crushing.

"Why didn't you tell us who you were?" He manages to spit out. I am sure there were spaces for expletives in there. He really isn't trying. I smile antagonising him further.

"You didn't ask." All pretence of giving a shit gone. I sip at the sweet tea that the nice Duty constable brought me.

"By wasting our time the real killer is getting away." He is exasperated. Poor wee lamb.

"You lot couldn't fall out of a boat and hit water." I sneer, it isn't really an attractive look. "Get me a lift back to Gleninch, and I wont mention the level of ineptitude you managed to display."

He is going red to purple from the collar upwards. Probably a stroke waiting to happen. He is trying to hold himself together but I am sure I can goad him past the point. Probably better not to.

"You are free to go. Your belongings will be returned to you." What a massive effort to retain control. He stalks from the room like Kevin the teenager.

"Thank you." I slurp my tea. I am so childish at times, it is embarrassing. They started it defence is probably not going to wash. I expect the Bishop won't be happy either.

Chapter 22

It was making me feel sick. The air was charged with mojo but whose it was I had no idea. After being vomitous when my room was attacked, I was wary of being so exposed. Of course, I was armed and not with mundane protection either. I had some Holy Unction in my pocket for my direst need. A little pukey feeling wasn't direst need, yet.

"I can feel you, you bastard." I mutter to myself. I try to keep the hostility to myself but I'm sure I just look like a grumpy git. The civic reception is to celebrate sixty years of new town status is not the place for a bun-fight. It is only three days since I had a run in with the Police in Falkland, and I don't think I am quite recovered from the ear bashing that the Bishop gave me over the rank stupidity of the situation. Worse still I had been fending off the attentions of Mrs Brookes and was running out of excuses, finally giving in to a meet tomorrow.

In the new council building, showing no end to the public money to be squandered is a gathering of the great and the good of civic society. Why on earth was I invited? Must be the dog-collar-factor. It gets me into all sorts of places. Some of them quite entertaining. Despite the nausea, I have a flute of fizzy white wine in my hand as I am introduced to the Lord Lieutenant of Fife and the Lady Provost. 'My, what a big gold chain you have Provost' is what I want to say but I stick to playing nicely with the other children.

"I'm a native." I pause to allow the Provost time to keep up and nod. "I went to school here and my sister still lives here." I sip, giving her a chance to chime in.

"Really?" She fakes interest so well. She is destined for high office, if her insincerity is a measure. Of course she isn't a native being from another part of Fife, Dunfermline. It might as well be another planet. Fife is a bit like that; if you aren't local then near enough isn't good enough.

"Oh yes, it's changed quite a bit over the last twenty years." Always helps to establish one's local pedigree and credentials. Prevents one looking like a total junket hog.

"What brings you back here Father Steel?" Oh dear, I knew someone would ask. I could get into a helluva trouble with this one. I will play it with the official line; a straight bat as they say.

"Sadly, Father MacPhail's demise brought me home. It has been a while." Look at that. Bland drivel and so in keeping with the occasion. Funny how that seems to work so well. I still don't know why my spidey-senses are working overtime. The room is full of the suited and booted and the addition of alcohol hasn't really worked. Although maybe I should try having more?

"Oh yes, a real loss to the community, so involved with everything. A real man of the cloth." The Lady Provost spouts the commonly held belief. Oh how little they really know. Of course, some in here really knew MacPhail for what he was. There are enemies all around, hidden in plain sight. Am I Julius Caesar surrounded by knife wielding plotters? I wonder if the Enemy knows that I am here. I manage not to splutter in my flute. I mumble platitudes to pass off my agreement with the accepted public image of the departed.

"Will you be staying long Father?" She asks as she sips her wine. She has piercing eyes, I finally notice. A lovely shade of blue, she must have been exceptionally pretty as a young woman.

"Not too long, I expect, only until a permanent replacement is appointed. Then my path will take me onwards again." Was she too interested? Or was it just politeness? The Provost's chain looks heavy but is obviously not real gold, just gilt. A veneer just like the town itself. New and civilised but underneath a whole different ball game; drugs, drink, satanic cults – you know, the usual 21st century problems. Luckily, an aide takes her elbow and steers her away from Tufty the Priest. "Lovely to meet you" exchanged with smiles. Yet neither smile reaching the eyes, what a pair of phoneys we are.

I drain my flute and turn to the conversation on my left where the Lord Lieutenant has been engaged by a sycophant of some sort. My head is still thudding dully and I am still no closer to identifying the source of my pain. I scan surreptitiously as I snag another cheap plonk from the drinks waiter.

This feeling of 'something not right' turns into a full-blown 'turn-the-fuck-round-now'. I always like to see the white of my enemy's eyes. Like a western gunfight, it's the eyes that matter. Easier to catch the bastards eh? I slowly look round, there at the far side of the room, a pair of eyes is boring holes into me and he's just too slow to look away in time before I clock him. Gotcha.

He's a normal looking bloke, pretty nondescript, is he a flunky or a dignitary? Nice suit though, grey with a shadow stripe, his tie is a blood red from a power dressing manual. Gold watch peeking out from French cuffs and natty cufflinks, thirty something so probably not a flunky. I keep an eye on him and those he is in conversation with. He knows I have clocked him and keeps trying not to look in my direction. Quite amusing really, or it would be if this wasn't serious.

Fuck it, I'm going in. Red leader standing by, I'm making my run now. I extricate myself from the Lord Lieutenant and the ass kissing that is going on. I can't exactly charge over and put the cross on him or drag him before the Inquisition, so I meander with purpose. Finger buffet and a fresh glass of wine (red this time) and I toddle over. Like a lioness stalking a gazelle, I am closing in and I can see his panic beginning to mount.

He tracks my progress and knows I'm coming. Better still he knows I know he's the enemy. He knows he might be up shit creek without a paddle. I can almost hear the jaws theme playing as I glide through the gathering. Above his collar a flush is starting to show, his discomfort becoming evident. Funnily enough I no longer feel nauseous, the feelings of moments ago have gone. Was he just being used as a channel for someone else? His master perhaps? The mojo has gone for now.

"Father, let me introduce you" a calm voice moves alongside me, pulling me into the group containing minion-of-the-dark-in-the-nice-suit. Here we go, chocks away and all that. I look round to see who's doing the steering, one of the faces from my flock apparently. The name escapes me as I let him lead me in. At least I hope he's one of mine.

"This is Councillor Gray, Councillor McIntosh, Councillor Swan and Councillor Dempster." He allows me time to shake each hand in turn and I look for my enemy but he has melted away. Shite and buckets of it. I know what he looks like, I'll get him.

"Councillors, I am pleased to meet you." I manage to keep disappointment hidden from my voice. Next time I'll get the slippery little flunky, nice suit and all. My vibrating pocket extricates me from a long, tedious conversation around planning objections for a new housing estate to the west of the town. Thank you, I almost mouth to the ceiling. Bishop Andrew is identified as the caller.

"Steel." I can't help myself, voice flat and neutral. I'm in public and giving nothing away. He is used to it, however.

"Andrew, that book is very important, can you come over this evening?" Wow, that is direct by any standard. For Bishop Michael, it is positively rude.

"Of course, I can be there by seven." I am interested to know what it is for, so my usual surliness is put on hold. It is a classic quid pro quo or something like that.

"See you tonight." He hangs up, no love and kisses or anything. I return to the function room, realising that I am probably marginal for being over the limit for driving later. I'd better eat some of these delicious looking sausage rolls, and the rather dubious looking wrap things with unidentifiable contents.

At the appointed hour I am pulling in to the gravel drive of supreme crunchiness at Bishop Michael's residence. I managed to have a little nap, later in the afternoon and let the three glasses of wine make their way through and out of my system. The stone building, housing probably, the most important Bishop in the UK (at least in the war against evil) is somewhat unremarkable but very old. The stone a welcome home for much of the lichen and moss that adorn the surface. The windows, old and leaded are very pretty but a bit too Gothic for my tastes. Anyway, I am here, as summoned.

Leaving the orange flashing hazard lights in my wake as the immobiliser kicks in on my hot little red number, I walk swiftly to the large door to the Bishop's mansion. It opens as my feet reach the steps. Like magic, I am easily amused, the personal assistant with the sour expression welcomes me to the residence. I bare my teeth at him. Apparently, I am to go right on in. A feeling of deja-vu settles upon me as we have meeting round two with Father Jeremy and his Eminence. I knock and enter in response to the bellow from within.

"Andrew, so glad you could make it. I have taken the liberty of having dinner prepared and plated for you." He motions to a wooden sideboard, upon which sits a dinner. With some sort of decorations around the edges, oh they are green beans. Far too healthy looking but I will have no choice but to devour it. I make my way over to the table where Jezza and the Bish are already ensconced.

It all looks so civilized, like three clergymen meeting for a meal. Well, on the surface that is what it is, it looks ordinary. It's not like this scenario is played out all over the world whenever a few dog collars are gathered together. Father Jeremy seems to be a bit more sociable as he sips a half-full goblet of claret. I look down at my plate, I know I will need to make an effort. Some meat substance in dark gravy, spuds, green beans, it is proper food. The Bishop smiles at me as I start to eat, I have no idea why. I notice he hasn't poured me a glass of the wine yet.

"Andrew, Father Jeremy has been looking at the book. Wherever did you find it?" Bloody pointless question as I have already done this with him on the phone. I manage not to let my sarcasm genes kick in. It must be for Father Jeremy.

"Under a warded floorboard, in the stair cupboard in the manse wrapped in velvet, Bishop." Perfunction at its best. No add ons. Sticking to the facts as I force down the green beans. I hate vegetables and I blame school dinners of the seventies. They were boiled to death until only a tasteless pulp was left; no wonder kids left them most of the time. A glass of Claret has appeared as if by magic.

"Andrew, it is a Grand Grimoire. Only a few of these have ever been recovered." Father Jeremy seems quite excited. I would have been concerned as it proves these guys are serious.

"Which means?" Bishop Michael, gets in before I do and I keep eating. Playing catch up without looking like I am gulping it down. 'Chew Andrew' my mother used to chide me about the rate at which food disappeared.

"It means, your Eminence, that the book gives us an insight

that we rarely get. These cultists are no amateurs but a well established and very powerful group." Full of good news I see.

"It seemed to me that there was a dark well of power underneath the manse." Bombshell dropped as I shovel in some more green beans. Both of their heads spin towards me, any faster and they would have had whiplash injuries. I chew on, keeping my mouth tight shut. 'Andrew chew with your mouth closed' was another one I heard regularly.

"There was also a blood worked circle in the lounge, which I started the walk back on. There have been a few pieces of work in that manse." I pick up my claret to have a swig, helps when giving bad news I suppose.

"Andrew, you need to share these things earlier." The Bishop doesn't look impressed. First he doesn't want detail and now he does. Seems picky to me. I do wish he would make up his mind.

"Bishop, I need to visit this manse. There is so much we can learn there." Father Jeremy is all bright eyed and bushy tailed it seems. The bishop is refilling his glass, me too I almost add but think he might not be too happy. Wait until he offers I think.

"Andrew?" He's asking me if I want to take Jezza on a field trip? I decide that I might as well go with the flow and assent. If the Bishop decides I need help I won't be able to refuse.

"Not an issue for me, as I need to complete the walking back of the circle. It isn't a nice place though." I try not to make it sound exciting. Jezza is licking his lips. I hope he will mop up the drool.

"I can come through at the end of next week if that works? I will need a few days to check the previous incumbents and the records. I should be back from Canterbury by then.' I shrug, I don't really care as long as he tells me when he wants to visit.

"It is settled then. Father Jeremy shall visit the manse and we shall take it from there." Bishop Michael tinkles his bell and the dinner fairies will be on their way. Better get on with my dinner and the claret. Have I been stitched up? Probably.

Chapter 23

Sometimes, I don't know why but I get a hankering to just check. You know, personally. That is why I am standing, in the cold, outside the back door of St Margaret-in-the-fields, checking that it is locked. Funnily enough, it isn't. The night is quiet as a tomb and so is the church. So why am I anxious? This door is not overlooked by any of the nearby houses and has easy access without being seen. A thick beech hedge runs down to the main road, offering good cover. An army could march up here and no one would be any the wiser. Okay, maybe not an army but you get the point.

I turn the handle and silently the door slips open. More a case of secret entrance and well-oiled hinges. The hairs on the back of my neck start to stand up, screaming a warning. A heavy drape blocks out any light from inside. I push the drape aside and let the door close behind me. This short passage runs along to the priest's dressing room, funny how I missed it. Hidden in plain sight and all that. It is always surprising what is missed by familiarity or just not seeing it as important. I don't usually have any qualms about entering the house of god but tonight it feels somewhat different. Yes its late, yes I'm sneaking in and yes some shit is going on. Oh for Brotherton and his pockets, or more specifically his torch. I can see the mat but that's about it. At least it doesn't say 'God lives here.' I smirk at my own humour. I should know better but with a dimple in my cheek I slip past the drape and step inside. Shutting the outer door behind me I drop the snib and let Yale guard my back. I may be suspicious but I don't like unlocked doors at my back. I've seen way too many Hammer House of Horror films. I am still not taking any chances, however.

A deep breath later and its time to go. I am a peeker. I like to peek first. I am not about to announce my presence until I know what or who else is here. It always pays to know what kind of shit you are about to step into. The hair on the nape of my neck is caressing and telling me to leave; or at least be careful. I am stuck in that minute between the moments that define everything. I take a breath and pulling up my big girl panties, move into the house of God.

The short corridor, which I am standing at the end of, turns after a few steps. I know this because the office is on my left. I can see light around the corner. Well, I can't see round corners but I can see that a flickering light is round there. Candle apparently. So, with my good sense running for the hills and my inbred stupidity taking over, I sneak like a ninja into the office. It is empty, thank goodness.

I consider calling Brotherton on my life saving cell phone but what would I say 'Brotherton, come quick I'm hiding in the office because there's a candle in the corridor?' Best not, I suppose. Maybe later.

It really takes no time for good sense to evaporate. I sneak, sidle, wall hug and crab-step along the carpet. Not a sound escapes my movement. Chuck Norris, eat your heart out. Wetting my fingertips, I reach down and snuff out the candle. It's a fat black one on a sturdy metal holder, another one further on lights the way. Awfully kind of them. I count the steps, just in case I have to run for it. Wouldn't want to crash into the wall after all.

As I get closer to black candle number two, I hear it. A low murmuring of voices, the words are indistinct but voices nonetheless. They are coming from inside the chapel itself. Is there a little ex-curricular evensong? I think not. As the incumbent, I most certainly do not approve. I could phone now but, like I said, stupidity should never be ruled out as a reason for doing something. Ninja-peeker that I am, I'm going to see who and what is going on. Although I could probably guess. Dennis Wheatley has furnished many a dullard with enough Satanist material to have a fairly good wild stab at it. Remarkably, they wouldn't be far wrong.

I should have run but I peeked through the partially open doorway. Safe in the darkness I have time to get a really good view of the proceedings. I'm a details kinda guy but usually miss the big things. Usually later I can re-picture and recall the whole thing but in the moment I can miss plenty.

I couldn't miss the fact that there is a whole gang of hooded and black robed folks in God's house. I didn't miss the fact that there has been some redecoration. Crux Ansata front and centre, altar has had a make over, its like a satellite TV house doctor show in here with faux fur throws and scatter cushions all over the floor. Oh yes and a pale skinned, rather fit, naked woman is spread eagled on the altar. See, I told you I miss things. Her head is hanging off the far end so I will have to wait to identify her. The incoherent mumbling still fills the air, no idea what is being said, probably Latin though.

"Brothers and Sisters" I practically jump out of my skin. One of them, with a phantom of the opera mask on, steps up behind the altar. It's show-time then. I hadn't expected a front row seat at the Satanic gathering of the month. My mind was rolling through significant dates on the calendar but I could hang this service on no saint day or significant day in the year. Perhaps this is just a weekly or monthly thing. It certainly doesn't fit with the known Satanic dates.

"Tonight we are gathered to feast. Before us is an offering to sustain us in our cause." He scans his little gang. I try to count them and get to about ten but there might be another one. A right dirty dozen. I wonder if he is the one who spiked my room. We'll see but I can't feel anything mystical or supernatural yet. Seems to be a load of middle class wannabes who want to dabble and get a little thrill. That and eternal damnation, obviously.

"Our Sister offers her flesh to bring us power; Our Master blesses us in our cause." He sweeps a hand over the altar and bows his head at the 'Our Master' bit. I find myself a little distracted by the view, she obviously waxes. I don't think it's cold either.

"Tonight, Our Master" (another nod), 'will fill us with power. The power to smite and drive away our enemy.' I presume he means me. I have never been the object of a special Satanic ritual; makes me feel kinda important. I doubt that he will be listening to their pleas. I am a little rapt by the show unfolding before me.

"Through lust give us power. Through Blood give us power and through deception make us strong. Let us erode the Latin Plague on the people of the Horned God." He has a powerful voice and a sense of theatre; he draws a curved blade across his forearm dripping blood all over her breasts. A sinister sight in the candlelight. With a swift tug at a cord his robe falls away. His mangy little flock do the same, hoods and masks still cover their faces.

Some images etch themselves indelibly on the mind, for me its nude women that have that effect. There are four I can see but now they are all moving around the altar. Car crash viewing at its best. I should leg it now but all my good sense left the building ages ago. They are moving round the altar counter clockwise, left hands entwined.

Their glorious leader, erect now, stands at the head end with his arms raised like horns as they pass round him. Like an adult game of ring-a-roses. They are mumbling again. If this were a Hollywood film then all the bodies would be toned and buff. It isn't and they aren't. Beer bellies and cellulite adorn the players. I am sure I have a Polaroid of a few of them somewhere. Are these just middle aged swingers with a twist? A new thrill? Well they're following enough clichés to be playing at it.

The smell of incense, same as I use, fills my nostrils as they start to caress the female offering. The excitement is building, if the male members are anything to go by, as they continue to circle. They bob (the men), and wobble (some of the women) as they build up pace, moving faster around the offering. The stroking and touching smears the blood all over her breasts, a mimic of a real sacrifice. Their symbolism is consistent, whoever is organising this is no fool. I feel a tightening band around my head. They are raising power, lots of power.

Through a gap in the flesh I see the Offering's mouth is filled with the Celebrant's member. Around the altar the pace picks up once more, they are circling faster and faster as he thrusts in time deep into her throat. One by one they genuflect and place their mouths on her freshly waxed genitals, her writhing testament to their facile tongues. I am distracted, never having actually observed a working, and should have left ages ago. St Margaret-in-the Fields has a satanic cult as a lodger. This has happened to churches before but this cult is for real. They are not playing at it, these aren't petty dabblers. This is a long established cult residing in the, rather ordinary, New Town Church of St Margaret's in the Fields.

I can feel the power of the sex magic thickening the air. It's almost like drowning or trying to breathe underwater. Closing my eyes and gulping in some air, I try to get control. They seem to be nearing a crescendo, only one of them is being filled with power I think. The Circle will get only earthly pleasure as a reward. The power is heavy and potent; making the darkness around me deeper and the pressure in my head feel like a vice.

I notice that they each stop to plant kisses on their master's behind as their circle spins. I like sex, I find it fascinating but this magic, sex and blood, is making me ill. I can't identify any of them and unless we have a naked Eucharist on Sunday, their identities are safe for now. I need to leave but I know I have waited too long. My feet feel like they are rooted to the spot and my legs like wood. I cannot leave now, even though I want to.

"Master" his supplication fills the room with power as he splatters the Offering's chest with his seed. It's like a thunderclap inside my head and I know I'm fainting. Fuck. Fuck, fuckitty-fuck.

Chapter 24

I am so foggy this morning that even the opening of my eyes is a Herculean task. I ache all over like a stampede of hairy highland cows has passed over me. Perhaps I had fallen asleep, or passed out pissed, on a drovers trail. I can't have been that pissed as I am undressed and in bed as opposed to the more traditional fully-clothed collapse on top of the sumptuously-soft motel bed. I have no recollection of anything, however.

The curse of whisky is the blackouts. The gaps in the memory and the inability to recall precisely what happened. Going by the strength of this hangover, a good night was, certainly, had by all. In fact, the lassitude that I feel would suggest a very late night was had and a further spell in slumberland is the order of the day. I blink at my wrist to find my watch has escaped and is just a few feet away adorning the bedside cabinet. I must have been utterly gone because I rarely take my chronograph off. Why I am so obsessed by knowing the time is a deep rooted psychological problem from childhood, I expect. That, however, would be the tiniest issue a psychologist would find if rooting around in my mind. It is not a place to explore for the uninitiated.

Everything feels so heavy as I seek to move across the bed to get my watch. My pubes are matted and my balls sticky. Not a pleasant sensation, so there was sex too? What a night to have no recollection of. This is so unfair, I am paying the consequence and I can't enjoy the sin. My bladder is telling me to move and if I know one thing, I know that it pays to obey. A few groans escape me as I lurch to the bathroom. The harsh strip light over the mirror lancing into my eyes and spearing my brain. My head feels like a split may occur any second. I am wrecked.

I sit on the throne, head in my hands and bemoaning my misery. Keeping my eyes shut is a good idea, I think. This is the emperor of all morning afters. What was I thinking? I readily admit I, probably, wasn't. What a bloody idiot. Even in this state I try to work out what appointments I have and what I can reschedule. It is now that I realise a piece of information is truly eluding me. What day is it?

Ablutions over, I look, through slitted eyelids, in the mirror. I look pale and this light isn't helping. Covering my chest is a series of bruises, and lower down too. There are more, low on my stomach and around my groin. Bruises? Love bites, what a blooming mess. A hungry vampire has suckled all over me and I can't recall a second of it. I have never had such a complete blackout covering events that I might have enjoyed. Something feels very wrong. Sharp, I am not.

The moment when realisation starts to dawn, is a horrible time. If I wasn't pissed then what the fuck happened to me? I need a shower, perhaps that will clear some of the aches and defog my brain. I doubt that it will but I will give it a go. A hot shower cascading and pummelling on my head as I stand immobile is slowly reawakening my cognitive functions. My arms are braced against the wall like Atlas I am shouldering a massive weight; the weight of ignorance and fear. A million what-if scenarios are buzzing around in my fevered imagination. My body has been used. How, exactly, I am unsure but spent would describe it pretty effectively.

Eventually I turn off the hot water and allow a moment of cold to caress me into life. Shock is a better description. It works and I step out on to the tiles, with the attendant little slip. I see my reflection and it is not a pretty sight. Neck hickies above the dog collar line, for fucks sake. I look down my reflection to assess the extent of my hickification. I count twelve on the front and one just at the base of my spine. Thirteen in all. Thirteen! A working, most definitely. How the fuck did that happen?

"Oh fuck." I start to check my body for aches, more specifically puncture wounds. I hope they haven't taken my blood. If they are amateurs then I might be lucky. They aren't and I'm not. I find a hypodermic puncture in my right arm. The size of this calamity is growing by the second. How on earth I will explain this to the bishop I have no idea. Impressed he will not be. I think that might be the least of my worries.

"You get me into so much trouble." I say addressing my penis and giving it a waggle. I notice a bald patch in the now de-matted pubes. Blood, semen, pubes – what else have they got? The shit-meter has gone into the 'very-deep' shit category. Meaning totally submerged in the shit storm to come. My demeanour is one of totally pissed-offed-ness as I scowl at my reflection. My phone ringing draws me from my staring contest. I shamble through to answer the call, my legs and hands not quite working but after only a few excruciatingly painful rings I manage to answer.

'Steel.' Just about, anyway.

"Andrew? Are you all right? You sound different." A pause, "Have you been drinking?" Bishop Michael worries that I will backslide again, bless him. He has every right to worry. When he rescued me, I had a whisky tolerance that would stun a rugby team and was heading to the very early exit from this life. With it would have gone the gift that God gave to me. Bishop Michael cleaned me up, well he had others do it but you get the idea.

"Yes, no, no." I am being unhelpful. It was three questions wasn't it? I could barely stand vertically as I slumped beside the bed, using it to stiffen my backbone and keep me semi-upright.

"What has occurred?" Bishop Michael continues. You or I would have said 'What has happened?' but Bishops aren't like the rest of us. They really aren't.

"I have been worked. I have no idea how or by whom. I need help." I sound tired, even to me. The words are slow and slightly slurred at the edges.

"Oh good gracious." He sounds shocked. See I told you they aren't like us. "Andrew are you safe?" An odd question.

"Well I have just woken up and had a shower." I begin at the beginning. "I am covered in love bites, have had multiple ejaculations, am missing a patch of pubic hair and have had blood taken." I pause. "Apart from that and no recollection of events whatsoever, I am just peachy." Too much detail? Probably. Now he knows as much as I do.

"Oh Dear Lord, Andrew. You might be in terrible danger. What can I do to help?" Wow, no questions about it being my fault. Supportive, I am unused to.

"I need purged and cleansed. Can you arrange it? Tomorrow, if possible." I need serious help, I need whatever they have done to me cleared up. I need the equivalent of 400cc of penicillin to clear the clap, and I need it soon. There is no shortcut to getting me out of this mess. There is no sure-fire way to break any hold they may have established over me.

"I will get it organised. I'll call you back." And he's gone, A Bish on a Mish, I laugh at the idea. I stop quickly as my head reminds me how much of a hangover I have. I flick on the television, in a vain hope that I can reconnect with the current date and time. A few flicks and the BBC tell me it is Tuesday and after one in the afternoon. Don't care about any of the headlines to be honest. I am blank on all of Monday and can only vaguely remember the Eucharist on Sunday. Well and truly wiped, then. Almost Men in Black standard, I haven't looked at any pens recently. I smile at my own humour.

Waking up naked, in a hotel room, covered in love-bites and having no memory of it sounds so rock and roll. Not exactly the sort of thing that the seminary prepares you for. My buzzing, noisy friend calls me back to the here and now.

"That was quick." I am almost happy sounding. Relieved probably.

"Listen Nazarene, we have you. We own you. Get out now, or else." Menace successfully delivered. I feel a cold chill run over me. Goosebumps and my hair standing on edge evidence of a change in temperature. Being naked and slightly damp may be a factor but I doubt it. I am in deep.

"Who is this?" When in doubt, be indignant. A very British response. It often throws people off their stride, not today though.

"Feeling cold Priest? What about now?" I feel a flush of

heat emanate from the centre of my back and roll round my body. A cruel laugh bursts from the phone.

"You are ours. Leave or die." The final words spat out and full of malice. I am truly worried now. I can just about see the sadistic sod playing with his effigy of me. Coated in my blood, semen and hair. What's next? A pin in the doll making me scream in agony. I pick up my rosary, wrapping the beads around my right hand. I need to respond, last word syndrome. It has often gotten me into trouble but I need it now.

"I don't think so. Do your baddest." Anything can happen now as I await a pain that doesn't come. Instead a stiffening in my groin as my flaccid friend starts to grow. I can't believe it. Whatever he is doing controls my very function. In a few heartbeats I am at full mast. I need to break this link. I hang up.

"Like hell you will." I am not giving in to these bastards. I begin to recite the creed of Nicea, the core articles of all our faiths. I regain control of my body. Now I am truly worried. The Bishop better hurry the fuck up.

Chapter 25

It sounds so nice, Cleansing. Like some sort of new age tai-chi bollocks. It isn't. It leaves me drained and emptied out. I don't know what they did to me and after this I will know. Well, actually, I will get the joy of re-experiencing it again. I haven't needed a cleansing in the last decade. It's not like a nice cosy confessional with an 'Ego te absolve' kind of thing. Oh well, the car is here and the roller coaster ride is about to begin.

When I told Bishop Michael to hurry up, he was as good as his word and the car has taken less than an hour to turn up here. It is a big black Volvo, all utilitarian and efficient. The leather seats look nice though. It isn't the Bishop's official car, more a workhorse for days like this. The driver nods as I get in and we are off. He says nothing as I sit and mumble my way through a few prayers. I want to keep control until I am safe. Bastards have really spooked me out. While I might look calm to the outside, my innards are doing a tango.

I feel a caress over my skin. I am alone but know they are trying to reconnect the link. Sex magicians then. They seem to know how to work inside my defences. I have faltered in my recitations of holy creeds and they have reconnected. Fuck. I bite my lip and the sharp pain clears my mind momentarily, just enough to begin again. The fact that I am moving is probably helping me escape their grasp.

I mumble louder and it seems that my mumbles are connected to the accelerator as the car speeds along the new link road, no screaming fan-belt, more a powerful growl as we pass car after car. We seem to be doing about a hundred miles an hour. I appreciate his candour but I want to get there alive. The bridge over the Forth is under our tyres and the attempted link is gone. Rivers, it seems, are a barrier that works on more than vampires. I take a deep breath, hold then let it out. Relaxing one-oh-one in action. More like a knackered Thank God that's over but you get the idea. I collapse back against the leather every muscle sagging, seat belt holding me roughly in place.

It feels that in no time we have pulled in to the gravel drive and I am being escorted to the door. Magically the door opens as I put my foot on the bottom step, who knew it was magic. I smile at my own idiotic thoughts. The flunky holds the door for me. Even he looks worried.

"Father Andrew, you are to proceed downstairs immediately, all is ready for you." Proceed, what a formal load of nonsense. Go for Fucks Sake, Go. What are you a fucking policeman? I almost scream at him.

"Thank you." I so can't be arsed flunky-baiting. I have been through this before, so there are no surprises. The stairs down are stone and unadorned, a nice little spiral stairway to the underworld. Perhaps another world would be more accurate. Medieval looking and solid, they have seen many a priestly traveller and offer only a reminder that the Church is old and has many, many secrets.

As I reach the bottom I step into the modern world. A fully fitted out secret lair resides beneath the palace. The stone walls the only real reminder of the age of this place. In front of me a dark haired thirty-something Lady Doctor in her pristine white lab coat waits for me. This is very different from the last time.

"Father Andrew, remove all your garments then step over here, please." No small talk then? No screen either. Modesty it seems will not be required. She is new, to me at least, and she is all efficiency. She is pretty, however, and that always helps. The unpeeling of my clothes begins. I notice it isn't cold in the room, funny that. I am glad, for lots of reasons. She is waiting and studying my manly physique as I get undressed, she shows no emotion as I finally remove the boxers that cover my bits. Hands are designed specifically for covering one's bollocks when naked.

"Where do you want me?" A little levity never hurt. Is that a little twitch of her lips, a beginning of a smile? Nope, crashed and burned. She has a solid professional look that drives out my poor attempts at mood lightening but I will keep trying anyway.

"Arms out at shoulder height, legs apart at hip width, please." She is walking round now, pen flying on her clip board. I comply, as failure to do so might lead to worse things.

"I don't need to cough do I?" I think I am funny, apparently she doesn't. She is looking at the love bites with some sort of red light. A magnifying glass mystically appears and she is peering at me, closely.

'These are from thirteen different mouths.' She isn't speaking to me as she starts writing. She is frowning a little and writes some more. The rubbing sound of her sleeve on the clipboard sounds loud in the silence that fills this room. I can't even hear the hum of the fan on the computers.

"What?" I try to sound unconcerned, but fail miserably. I know that this is serious and I have been lucky to escape their grasp.

"There are hypodermic punctures in each one. As well as the one in your arm." She walks to the stainless-steel trolley-tray thing and returns with a swab thing and starts swiping over the hickies. She is very efficient and there is no stirring as she works near my groin, thank goodness. I jump as she unexpectedly lifts my penis and swipes all over it. It is bloody cold. The peeling of foreskin and swipe around is dispassionate and I focus clearly on a speck on the wall.

"This will smart a bit." She is still holding my Penis and she isn't kidding. The heat from the insertion of a rod into my urethic opening is unpleasant and requires a deep breath. That was only half of it; the scraping of the little umbrella is intense.

"You will need treatment for all known STDs just in case, but this swab will identify any actual infections." Oh joy of joys, just what I need. Serves the little fella right; he has been getting me into trouble for years.

Anyway she lets go of my now brutalised member and stands before me, light test on my eyes and a few other doctor like things. I tune out as she concludes her examination, which involves a few utterly pointless pokes and prods. She brings a camera over and the flash startles me. I wasn't expecting that.

"I hope you got my good side and zoomed in." I try to be funny but fail, once more. I sound like I have body issues, which I don't but I don't want full frontals of my body being posted anywhere. Not even in her Occult Doctors Quarterly.

"I have zoomed in on the bruises for reference purposes. Your modesty is safe Father." She smiles gently with a little imp-like dimple. Not an Ice maiden after all. She is pretty and underneath I can feel her sympathy for my ordeal. She hands me a paper suit onesie to wear and points to the door.

"The Bishop will meet you in there soon."

In my white paper onesie, I make my way through a rather ordinary looking door into a stone hewn corridor leading to a private chapel. Who built this and when I have no idea, but it is old and the paper feet are doing nothing to keep out the chill. It is a holy place, and one where many have prayed (and probably received) divine inspiration. I hope so. It is here that I will begin the process of my cleansing. Upon the wall a crucifix, looks down at me and I can feel the emanation from it. Power, pure power for good. A few kneeler mats lie against the rough wall and the candles that illuminate the room are fat and white, proud on plain wooden holders sunk into the floor.

"Andrew." The bishop joins me. His voice filling my ears but not loud enough to be a shout. The tone is formal and serious. This is not a routine thing and we need this to cleanse me of their influence.

"Bishop." Great small talk. In fact I don't want to speak in here, it seems wrong somehow. This is not a room for idle chatter and pointless words. I turn round and see that he has brought a jug and cup. Obviously water. He hands them to me, genuflects to the Crucifix and leaves. He will be back at dawn, when the long night has been passed.

I will be alone in here, with water and nothing else until tomorrow where my excoriation will begin. I have time to reflect and time to come to terms with what has happened to me. I strip off the paper onesie and select a padded kneeler. I approach the crucifix with eyes downcast and position myself at his feet. The plain red kneeler, the colour of blood, in recognition of his gift of sacrifice will have permanent dents after this I expect. My usual irreverence is stowed away as I contemplate the sacrifice of our Lord and the ordeal of the cross.

The long night has begun and I silently begin to pray. I know that this connection and sanctuary will be vital in removing the enchantment laid upon me. It is only by reaching a purifying zen-like state that I will be able to move forward. The silence is crushing and my ears can pick out the tiniest flickering of sound from the candles as they mark the passage of time. The early onset numbing through my knees is another measure. I used to be able to stay kneeling for hours at a stretch but nowadays the discomfort sets in early. I will need to change position early and often. Middle age and all that. It isn't the age it is the mileage.

I hope that by silencing the worldly noise and bustle I will be able to find memories locked deep inside of what was done to me. By finding out what they did I will be able to work against them. So far the numb knees are pulling my attention and making that inner silence difficult to find. I wonder if I should lie down? Perhaps not. I drink the first cup of water from a pewter cup and wonder how often this is used or is it a special cup for those who need this place.

Everything slows and the silence becomes total. While I may indeed be an irreverent wise-ass, this place is one which truly removes any desire to be so. I reconnect my body, my thinking and embrace the power that has grown in this place over the years. Holy men have prayed here, and I am the least of them. The redemption of the sinner is for those like me. My acceptance is total but then again, I have proof everyday of the eternal struggle of Good and Evil, so it is a simple matter really. I try to roll back the steps and actions of the past few days, from arriving here and the journey over in the car to the discovery and hopefully I can extract something from this fog.

Sounds come to me, not pictures yet, and it is as if I am muffled and only maddening little half word sounds are crawling out of my memory. Perhaps I was hooded? That might explain it. I try further back to find an image or a feeling. It feels like an age has passed when I am startled by an image. Vivid and sharp.

She is above me, masked, and riding my cock as I am held down. There are many hands holding me. Blonde hair spills past her phantom of the opera mask and her rather fantastic figure is a sight to behold. There is some chanting going on too. I jump, as if shocked to see this event of my recent past and then ephemeral it slips away from me and try as I might it will not come back. It wasn't Angela Brookes though, the breasts were totally different. Very nice, but different nonetheless.

Chapter 26

All through the night, I try and try to pull out more memories but there is a very definite hand brake there. A wall if you will, and only one look beyond this barrier was afforded me. Even then it was a fleeting, tantalising little glimpse of little real use in identifying any of the cultists. I hope it was a real memory and not a composite of fantasy. He isn't known as the prince of deception for nothing. I try not to fight to catch the image that is just out of reach.

The water is long finished and a drouth (as they say in these parts) is upon me. I am thirsty, sore and bloody knackered. The candles are guttering and making a racket. My heightened senses identified that the candle nearest the door has just gone out. All is now dark, or are my eyes closed. Who knows? It is the former as I try to stare around the room. What time or day it is I have no real idea, except that the Bishop will return at dawn for me. I hope he doesn't sleep in.

Often as one sense is denied another takes over, or so they say, I stare deep into the blackness of the chapel. Amazing what you can see when there is no light. Another little glimpse is coming, I can feel it. Tantalisingly close now, almost able to taste it. A thunderous noise behind me as the door is pulled open, jolts me back to the here and now. As loud as the rolling away of the stone that sealed the tomb of Our Lord. The flooding light searing my eyes ending my Long Night.

"Behold, I am the Light!" The Bishop's voice is strong and full of power. Who knew the old dog had that in him. "Andrew, return to the light. Night is passing. It is a new day. Walk in the light with the Lord.' His crook in one hand and his hand outstretched to take mine. Like a little lost sheep returning to my shepherd, I rise and stumble towards him. A rebirth, as it were.

Now begins the scouring and cleansing of my soul and the physical vessel in which it resides. Holy unction adorns my brow, the fingers of the Bishop making the sign of the cross, forever marking me as one of God's flock. The ring proffered to my lips is kissed swearing fealty to God and his church on earth. His benediction calls the blessing of the Father, Son and Holy Spirit on this poor strayed prodigal. I can feel the heat suffuse my limbs and fill my heart with joy. Who says there is no magic in this earthly world? It is here all right. We seem to have lost the means to find it.

I follow his crook as he leads me to another room with a massage table whose legs are set into the floor. Four Priests come forward and lead me to my position. Face down with manacles holding my naked body to the table. It is about to begin. My face can see the floor and the padding is almost comfortable. I know what is next so I am anything but relaxed. Excruciating it will be. The driving out of any evil ties to me will take time and involves making the host body so uncomfortable that the malice is driven out. In the middle ages whips and chains would have been de rigueur, thank goodness for progress.

Silence reigns for a second and then eight hands full of coarse grained salt start to rub all over my back, legs, shoulders and buttocks. Which might have been simply uncomfortable soon becomes unbearable as they scour and scrub my tender flesh. There are no areas exempt from this harsh handed rubbing and before long I realise it is my voice I can hear screaming in agony. There seems to be no stopping and this is only the back. My face and genitals will be subject to this too. I just want it to stop and stop soon. Sweat is running down my face and dripping off the tip of my nose. There are tears running just as quickly, even though my eyes are scrunched shut. Searing heat is running from my feet, all the way along my body as my feet are being treated now. I would have told everything by now, had there been questions to answer.

Limp as a dish-rag, I lie there whimpering, sobs racking my chest as I can't get a breath. For how long I lie there, I have no idea but I am being turned over and my respite is over. They begin again. I don't know if it is worse to see my brothers of the cloth rubbing and sweating as they labour over my flesh or to have had the view of the floor. I try to focus on the ceiling but soon I am floating on a sea of torment as nerve endings all over me scream in protest at the treatment of salt. Dead Sea salt, apparently, the only suitable salt for this job. Dark Magic doesn't like it, so rumour states. I know I bloody don't. All at once the restraints are loosed and I curl foetus-like and sob my way to insensibility.

Strong hands raise me from the table and carry me, unresisting and barely conscious, to another place. I am lowered into an ice bath that almost causes my heart to stop. My throat constricts and I cannot pull air into my lungs. Never mind the sensory overload that is assaulting my brain. A long silent scream passes my lips and my rigid body is held tight. The bumping cubes alongside my face are almost too much to bear. I am ducked under the water and I choke and splutter as my still open mouth fills with ice cold water. I am brought to the surface, cough and pull air in gulping like a landed fish. Under, again I am forced, as they hold me tight to the course. Thrashing and struggling in their grip, I am submerged again and again. The shivering is uncontrollable and I think my bladder has emptied. I am losing any connection to my body as the toll of the purging is paid.

I am pulled out of the water and the cold air feels even more so, as I am carried elsewhere. Chattering and chittering my teeth are battering off of one another. I will need dentistry if this keeps up. My neck and jaw aches from being clenched so hard. Actually there isn't a single part of me that doesn't register as being in pain. Even my hair hurts. I am a miserable wreck of a human being and I know we are not done yet.

After the cold, I am to be sweated. The steam room then sauna that the Bishop had installed is perfect for just this type of thing. You know, torture. While I am coming back to the land of normality from scrubbing and flash freezing, the steam room is almost unbearable and I know worse will come as I am taken into the hot box. Who knew removing enchantments was like treating a sprain. Hot and cold treatment until improved. The warming of my body is welcome as I stop shivering and the teeth have, in fact, survived. I am washed out and nearly catatonic. The Sauna is pulling sweat from my pores in rivers, making the salty fluid aggravate my sensitised nerve endings. I moan as my misery is complete. Would whips and chains have been better? If I have to do this again I will be asking.

It is bad enough to have been foolish and to have fallen between the sinful thighs of an adulteress. It is much worse to have confessed your actions to the Father Confessor, who looks like the very notion of any earthly pleasure, would be anathema. His disapproval really strikes home the levels of my stupidity and the need to be fulsome in my contrition is not in any doubt. My sins are many and the questions surrounding them are pastoral and about my relationship with The Almighty. No vicarious thrill seeking from this Priest, he is worried about my relationship with God and my self-destructive tendencies.

"Why do you resist the path that Our Father has laid before you? You have powers to use for the good of His flock and yet you rebel at every turn. You must seek the answer within yourself, my son." Buggered if I know might once have been my response but today after an exhausting night my witty responses have all vanished like a sale of Château Neuf de Pape in Tesco.

"The powers of darkness beset us at every turn and we aren't winning." I manage to mumble. My desolation after last night is almost all consuming. The building blocks of my Id have been disassembled and are now down to me to reassemble.

"My Son, the powers of the Enemy that assail us are as nothing before the power of our Heavenly Father. Your trials and tests are harsh and rightly so." His sympathy for my burden, is appreciated but I don't quite get where he is coming from. My silence leads him on.

"Faith, that is the difference." He stops, and waits. I am

meant to join the dots myself. It is a struggle. Maybe my ordeal has left me slightly slow. It seems that the lack of a need for faith, having proof already, is the root of my behaviour. I know that the Almighty exists, no doubt. Absolute knowledge. Most people struggle with uncertainty and that leads to undesirable behaviours. My problem is that I know I am already in the shit up to my ears so take a somewhat cavalier attitude in my actions. He tells me that I abuse this knowledge like a spoiled child. He is right but I don't really want to be told such. I will have, I don't doubt, hours of penance to do before I am absolved. I wait for the sentence and wonder just how many our Fathers or Hail Mary prayers will be needed.

"Ego te absolve a peccatis tuis." The magic words wiping my slate clean, once more. I am utterly stunned that he has decided my repentance is complete at this stage. There is more but I have paid my penance and now can be on my way. If only it were to be so simple. I have a couch session to go yet, more self analysis and a great big dollop of angst. Freud will be sitting in, analysing my bloody awful relationship with my mother.

Chapter 27

Dim light, a nice soft leather couch and another person in the room, not in my line of sight but I know they are there. Obviously it's time to talk about my mother. Or perhaps it's my childhood and my early fumbled sexual encounters. I have, what can only be called an overriding, contempt for psycobabblists, or whatever they are are known as. Psychoterrorists, or something like that. Analyse that. Fuck's sake there's elevator music coming from somewhere. Now, over the last 12 hours or so I have been broken down to my most basic level and wrung out. Stomped by a herd of theological elephants and scoured to within an inch of my sanity, and now I have to endure a session of this nonsense.

"You know that psychoanalysis doesn't work on the Irish, they are immune." Let's start with a joke and play nice. I try to take the tension from my voice.

"Father Andrew, it says here you are Scottish, from Fife. Not Irish." A humour bypass in action. A woman though, so all looking up a bit. I much prefer spilling my guts to a woman. Although she won't understand the half of it.

"Really? Who knew." I stare up at the ceiling anyway. If I am expecting some sort of inspiration from the emulsioned surface above me I might have a very long wait.

"Do you know why we are talking?" She asks gently. I wondered that very thing myself. As far as waste of time goes, psychoanalysis is right up there as far as I am concerned.

"Because silence is difficult?" I really can't be arsed. Let's see where that goes. I wonder if my notes say churlish and childish.

"'Is silence difficult?" Oh For fuck's sake. I wait, surly child time. She must have a great deal of patience or be being paid by the hour at an exorbitant rate to put up with this.

"We are trying to unlock your memories and see if we can discover what happened when you were under an enchantment." She is taking no shit from me, might just be calling her Ma'am by the end. It might be just what I need.

"Shall we begin?" Not really a question more a command, couched like I have a choice. The muzak goes off. A period of silence descends over the space between us. "What is the last thing you remember before the black out?"

"Locking up the vestry and heading back to my lousy travel Inn. Where I woke up later." I pause. So does she. I am to continue, obviously.

"No wait I don't think that's right." I am surprised because I am trying to remember and I think I constructed that from what I should have been doing. "I remember something else. A blue car that nearly rear ended me at the roundabout. He was shouting until he saw the dog collar. That was on the way back from Eucharist." Wowsers, how much has been wiped?

"OK, lets try something. It is a deep breathing exercise. It will create an environment in which we can dig deeper. Breathe in for seven counts and out for eleven counts. We will do this for twenty repeats. Begin." I presume the we, is so I don't feel a pratt. She won't be doing them with me. I start the count. I doubt I will manage to keep track. Twenty is a lot of fingers, might need to take my socks off. I start, as she breaks the silence, her voice probably no more than a whisper. She is close by and it is wholly dark. Have I dozed off.

"It's time. Let's walk our way forward from the car incident.' Her voice is soft and runs into my ears like desert sand.

"These are things that are passed and can harm you no more. Release the memories from the prison you have built to keep them from you." She slides on and lets the words sink in.

"I built the prison?" I am somewhat incredulous. If I wasn't so chilled out I might object. I feel that arguing is so not worth the effort and I let it go.

"It's your mind. You decide what you remember and what you forget. Open the door and look inside. These memories cannot hurt you. They are passed." She stops and waits again. The darkness and quiet seem somehow a comfort to me.

I choose to forget do I? Well that's a new one. I try to recall what happened after the arse in the blue car. Nada, zip, hee-haw.

"Imagine if you can a prison door, locked before you." She waits, assuming I am compliant. "Look down at your hand, see the keys. Put the key in the lock. Turn it and open the door." I try. A medieval dungeon door stands before me and in my hand I have a big fucking black iron key, I insert the key and turn. By God we are in.

I don't know if you have seen the matrix but like Neo I am flying like superman through a battery of mundanity that filled the hours of my day that Sunday Afternoon. For some reason, I wanted to check out the church that night. What was I thinking? No idea, but then again it might come to me sooner or later.

I watch in vivid HD technicolour the satanic working and the coven's enjoyment of their naked sacrifice. I remember passing out as the Celebrant splattered his jism all over the naked breasts of the willing hottie. I also remember the floor coming up to greet me as I passed out. What on earth was I doing waiting that long? What happened next?

"Can you recall anything since the blue car?" I hear her voice coaxing me forward. I am not inclined to explain the movie I have just watched, especially not the full on naughty bits.

"Yes. There was a satanic working in the church and I passed out." Minimalist stuff, eh? Would it be worth mentioning the oral sex or the hot sacrifice on the altar? Probably not needed this time. I am sure she really doesn't need to know.

"Then what Andrew? This next bit is important." Her voice is like smooth oil sliding across my skin under soft hands. Is she a mystic too? I wonder. It seems I want to tell her though. It is like a brain massage under gentle fingers.

"I am lying on the altar." It's pouring out now, I can't and don't want to stop it. Like a pus boil, it needs squeezed until it's all gone. This is the poison that was set in my system.

"They are all around me, chanting and I can't move. They are holding me down. They are aroused and excited and even though they have masks I can feel their fervour." I am so coherent it surprises me. It is like I am detached and removed from these memories, dispassionate, almost. The censor has left the building, taking my embarrassment with it.

"I am unresisting, I think. They have undressed me." I feel it necessary to explain I am nude on the altar. "I am fondling the genitals as they circle past. I don't think I am in any sort of control. The actions are wooden and like I am a puppet." It seems as if I was the second course of sex magic on that evening.

"You have done nothing wrong. Focus on what was going on. Details, if you can." She prompts gently, and I want to deliver, her goodwill all that matters just now. It is like I need her approval and assurance that I am guiltless on this. I was the victim and it isn't a role I play well.

"They are caressing me, getting me ready for sex." I can feel my blushes starting even now. I know I was not in control but I am still embarrassed. I need to carry on with this.

"One of the fatter women has mounted me, rubbing her slick pussy all over my face. I am writhing trying to get away." I hope I was trying to get away anyway. There are so many of them and my body is overwhelmed as I am the object of their sexual attack.

"There are hands and mouths all over me as she is grinding on my mouth. I am being ridden too." I am not telling the half of it but I am sure she understands that. Like any regression therapy, I am reliving the event and the tent in my trousers is a source of embarrassment for the future. I am so glad it is dark in here.

"Go on." No inflection, just a request. The silence that fills up the space between us feels long but is probably less than a minute as I pull myself through the ordeal.

"They are using me, I can't see who but there are a number of them. The one over my face is blocking any sight of what is going on. My body is betraying me repeatedly. I have no idea how long it is going on." I know that those using my member have been both male and female and I feel sick at the thought.

"Move forward, what next?" She is getting me out of there

and I appreciate it. I don't need to dwell in that place. I let out a long shuddering breath that sounds shaky, even to me.

"They are sucking me, all over." I guess that this is where I got the marks that so decoratively cover my flesh. Bastards.

"I can see the many heads buried against me." I am disconnected from the event. I see a face. One of them looked up as I looked down. I will know him next time. Got you, you bastard.

"My head is pulled back over the edge of the altar, I can't see anything. It has gone dark, I think I have been hooded." I lie. I am not telling anyone of the use of my mouth and throat by their Priest. Revenge is a deal best served cold. I will be cutting off his cock if I get the chance; law or no law.

"What can you hear?" She isn't letting me off that easily. She knows I am holding out and she is probing.

"Laughter. Cruel and harsh." They seem to have enjoyed my degradation. Like I said, vengeance is mine and it is coming.

Chapter 28

The buzzing sensation in my pocket was an unexpected pleasure. If only it would vibrate for much, much longer. I pull it out to see that Angela is the caller. No surprises any longer with modern technology, oh for the old days when a phone call was a mystery.

"Hello." I speak quietly into the microphone. I am not sure that I should do anything with her. My skin still glowing from the massive exfoliation a few days ago. I am almost back to normal but don't need this right now.

"'You need to meet me now." Her voice sounded a little strange. I decided to be gentle with the refusal. I need to keep my distance.

"Tempting, as it sounds, I have a few things to do today.' Playfully rejecting the offer of a nooner; you know lunchtime sex. After all I have been cleansed and it wouldn't do to fall at the first fence. I want to keep myself out of trouble.

"They'll hurt me if you don't." There are tears in her voice; changing the scenario from salacious to dangerous. I can feel the fury building in me, my vengeance has not been wrought yet.

Perhaps this is the first outing of my revenge on these bastards.

"Who will? Who has you?" I am already moving from the Priest's desk and on my way to the rescue, although I don't know where to go yet. If only I had a white stallion to ride in on.

"They will, you know who They are." Abruptly the receiver is pulled from her. The sound of force being used can be heard in the background. I feel my grip tighten on my phone, whitening my knuckles.

"Come on Priest, you don't want your playmate to feel the bite of my monster." A voice that spawned many sinister villains crawls out into my ear. This one sounds like the real deal, not the pretenders I have heard before.

"Where? When?" I spit into the phone. There's no point in denying Angela Brookes is important to me. I am asking myself how far will I go for her safety? After all she was one of MacPhail's partners too.

"Kirkcaldy. Old Sea-view car park. At the back overlooking the beach. We'll be waiting. Come alone." Cold, flat and obviously an utter bastard. What I will do when I get there I have no idea. It isn't like I can beat them up; not really my bag.

"I'll be there." I want to add 'you little shit' but Angela's muffled cry of pain distracts me. The line goes dead. My face contorts in that silent For Fucks Sake look. I really have no idea where we are going to go now. They have ratcheted up the level of threat. I must be getting closer to something. I have at best a tenuous grasp of what has been going on. Organ smuggling but a distinct lack of proof or a working hypothesis. Locking the church doors and extracting my car keys, I will soon be on my way to a dangerous liaison. Not the one I had expected just moments earlier.

Should I phone Brotherton? And say what? The Bastards have kidnapped my girlfriend and then have to cover all the disappointing details of my sordid affair. Fuck that. I will text him if I get into trouble. They aren't likely to kill me in broad daylight. Run me out of town maybe. I wonder what on earth they have in mind. Another knee in the nuts? A faint ache, as if in memory of the event, fills my stomach. I will be nice and compliant to get Angela out of danger. We can get even later. Revenge is a dish best served cold and all that. I am building up a banquet of paybacks for the future.

It is lunchtime so we should be fine, with other people about and using the car park. In a few minutes I am arriving in Kirkcaldy, birthplace of Adam smith and called the Lang Toun. It is so called because it is a long stretch along the coast looking across to Berwick Law and Edinburgh. I am summoned to the farthest end for a meeting that might just be fatal. I am hoping not, obviously. With a new link road the journey is a quick one and very soon I am cruising along the 'Prom' heading to the older, less salubrious, part of town. The sea-view car park is at the rear of a derelict old warehouse store, whose sign has long since been removed. As a nearly-local I know the way and don't need the help of a map. There has been a sprouting of little houses made of ticky-tacky for the young upwardly mobile professionals. These must overlook my meeting place and will be a source of witnesses if it all goes Pete tong.

I turn into the car park. Fuck it is deserted apart from one big black car at the far end, an SUV of some kind. I park slightly far away, deliberately. I don't want to get too close to them. A sunglasses-wearing, mean-looking, shithouse-shaped thug steps out of their car. He has been watching far too many mafia movies. He makes sinister, comical for me. He is glaring at me, I can tell. I get out and point my fob behind me. I take comfort in the noise it makes.

"You waiting for me?" I do my best Don Corleone but I don't think he gets it. Why is he wearing a polo neck sweater under a suit jacket? Maybe the shirt collars don't go up to his size. Of course he doesn't appear to have a neck, just a stump that is holding up his head.

"Get in Priest." Ooh that was so scary. I am all a-tremble. Well not really but I don't want to get in. After all once I do I am really in trouble.

"Let the girl go and I'll come with you. Where is she?"

Movie scripts one-oh-one.

He puts a phone to his ear and waits. His stare, at least I presume he's staring, looks ridiculous with the sunglasses. He just looks like a walking cliché. We stand like a pair of gunfighters, waiting. A car pulls in to the car park behind me; the crunching of gravel as it moves towards us confirms its approach. It parks beyond the SUV.

The doors open and Angela is led out. Her usually well turned out appearance somewhat dishevelled. The creasing on her upper arms shows signs of being held by some grubby mitts. Her face is a little pale but no runny mascara marks. Waterproof obviously. I give her, what I hope is, a reassuring smile. She gets a shove towards me and manages a stumble but not a fall. Her heels wobble a little but she manages to throw herself into my welcoming arms. I hold her for a moment and fill my nostrils with her scent.

"Let's go Priest." Well he is nothing if not consistent; dull but consistent. I hand Angela my car keys and whisper in her ear. "Contact Brotherton, he'll know what to do." She nods, almost imperceptibly, and hugs me for what may be the last time. I bloody hope not. Feels good to be held by someone who cares. Even if I should never have been there in the first place. Letting go of her luscious curves, it is time to uphold my end of the bargain. I make my way to soprano-boy. Oh well, here we go. A meeting with the enemy

"Get in, Priest." He rumbles again. I resist the urge to say 'I'm getting in, Thug, flunky or whatever you are.' This is heading in the wrong direction very quickly. I get in. The blacked out windows prevented me from seeing Flunky number two. He motions me to buckle up. In his lap a black balaclava with grey patches stitched over the eye area. I will be wearing it I presume. It will mess with my hair.

Neckless, as I now think of him, gets in the front. The hair cover is thrown into my lap and a get-it-on waggle of the pistol gives me instruction. Where the fuck did that come from? I hate guns, they have one function; killing people. Fuck. Flunky two seems to have a better command of language and doesn't have the Mafioso twang. I do as I am told.

The car starts and we are off. I sit still counting and breathing steadily. I know the area and will perhaps be able to get an idea of where they are taking me. We are at the junction, right and we are into Kirkcaldy left and we are off down the coast. I hear the indicator clicking and we have turned left, the coast it is. Excellent, I know the coast road well. I will, hopefully be able to trace my movements later, Brotherton will be so pleased. I am presuming there will be a later.

So off we go, a few bends and curves and after a few minutes (reached 300 on my count) we are indicating. Must be taking the

Kinghorn loch turn off, it's the only turn off. Bumps and corners confirm it, especially the very tight left-righter at the far end. Soon we are entering Burntisland, a lovely seaside town with attractions in the summer and crazy golf. I loved coming to Burntisland as a child, great trampolines too. I can almost see where I am. He slows to meet the speed limit, Neckless is a careful driver; we will arrive at a roundabout soon. Left down into the town, right inland and straight on up the hill to Aberdour. I get distracted and have lost count but I will start again after the roundabout. We go straight on, heading for Aberdour. All going well, might as well not have the balaclava on. Oh dear, what a bonus this might turn out being. I should be terrified but I am not, I keep focussing on where we are and not on the what might happen to me. I am, as they say, living in the moment. In the moment there is no place for the little death, fear.

Up and down the hill, slowing and through Aberdour we go, not stopping here either. I am less sure of the next bit but I think we have turned into Dalgety Bay. Not sure but we are sitting in traffic and not moving much. Straining and having lost count again, I need clues, anything. A tannoy announcement, what was that ' The next train arriving at Inverkeithing' So we didn't turn off into Dalgety Bay, soon we are winding through the streets of Inverkeithing with turns, left, right and we are in a housing scheme. We went sharply downhill so I know roughly where we are. We are here, apparently, the roller door of the automatic garage closes behind us. I will be able to find this again I reckon. You amateurs are so toast.

"Leave it on Father." The first words spoken for about half an hour. I leave it. Inside I am exultant, we have a location. Sort of.

It isn't a big house, feels like an 'ex-cooncil hoose' because in short order I am into the arena and sitting on an office chair. Duck tape wraps my arms and I await the arrival of the big boss. I strain my ears listening for clues not that my hearing is that great; I hope I am never blind. I hear footsteps and an outside door closing. The Balaclava is yanked off and a bright lamp shines directly into my face. White spots and a screwed up face time.

"What are we to do with you, Father? Any sensible man would have left by now." A slightly effeminate, lisping voice fills the silence. The hairs on the back of my neck are standing now. I feel cold, this is it. I go for bravado.

"Let me go? Wash my car? Get me a coffee?" Infantile, I know. I need to try and get the spots off the centre of my eyes and I squint and look from side to side. It probably doesn't really work, anyway.

"Sadly, not this time. Tell me, Father, why were you sent to replace MacPhail? It was no accident." I wonder where he is going. You don't kidnap someone just for this.

"Just Lucky, I guess." Hopefully I can irritate a mistake from him. I, usually, irritate everyone, eventually. Sometimes it can be really quick.

"Do not play the fool, Father. We are serious men and you would do well to cooperate." His softly spoken voice is seductive and dripping honey. I feel a little change in the spiritual ambience, he is gathering his will.

"That's me, Mr Awkward. Name, Rank and serial number." I grin at my own joke. I might be being silly but it is buying me time. Time for what I am not sure.

"Answer me." No change, just a compulsion. My eyes feel like they are being sucked forward. I can't blink, Fuck. I can feel them drying in the lamplight. I really want to blink but it seems that pulling them together is impossible.

"Father, why are you here?" The voice again. I feel the power contained in the undertones. I want to answer. I can feel my mind forming the answer. I have no idea what will come out.

"To catch MacPhail's Killer." I hear my own voice say. Bloody traitor. He has the upper hand now. I have complied once and refusing next time will be harder.

"There has been a confession for that crime already, you will leave when the replacement arrives." His suggestion feels all warm and comforting. On another person, this would have gained agreement but he has pushed too soon. I know the confession is hinky and it jars in my head. I wait. Clearing the fog is difficult.

"You want to go home and leave the whole thing behind, don't you Father Andrew." Oh he is good, though. Do I play along or frustrate him? I can't help myself, time to pop his balloon.

"It's the paperwork." I pause and blink. "You know, the forms, the reports. It is never-ending." The utter randomness catches him off guard. The link has been snipped. I can feel the cobwebs melting away as I straighten in the seat.

"What?" No syrup in his voice this time. He is annoyed and incredulous.

"I said the paperwork is horrendous." Surreal, python-esque idiocy. Deal with that matey. He can't get a handle on the lack of connection; he needed me to concentrate on his topic.

"Silence." His voice roaring like a lion inside my head leaves me gasping. Oh fuck. Perhaps I have pissed off the wrong chap.

"My master commands you Nazarene. Forget us. Begone. This is not your affair." The rushing of blood in my head has reddened my vision and my head feels like two taloned claws are crushing my skull. I must resist. In my head I scramble my thoughts.

"18, 42, 17, 26, 3, 9, 17, Baa Baa black sheep, cock, bollocks,

Sampras, Spain, Beckenbauer.'" I select utter randomness to thwart him. He has nothing to catch. I keep going with the randomness.

"You will obey!" Thunderous, painful and full of power. I scream in pain as the talons crush my skull, squeezing my brain. That is how it feels as his mind bears down on mine.

"Fuck you." I spit through tears of pain. Defiance my only weapon.

"Obey me! My master wills it." The current of his power is coursing over me. His anger is palpable and directed entirely at me. Why don't I have gifts like this? What did I get? Impressions and psychic shocks.

"Say please." I manage to grit my teeth.

"I command you, submit to my master." he is practically screaming in my face. His eyes bulging as he strains to dominate me.

"Never." Great dialogue eh? I wish I could have managed some thing pithy but I am drowning under waves of dark power. The air is charged. I wonder where the flunkies are, I am getting distracted. This episode may have been going on for minutes but I feel like I have been working out for hours. I am weary, already. A door behind us opens. The air clears as my enemy has lost his focus. I can feel a trickling bead of sweat crawl down my spine. My hair is plastered to my forehead. The clamminess holds my clothes against my body as I realise that the sweat covers my whole body.

"Let me." A new voice greets me, bland and quiet.

"Of course, Master." I can feel the expectant triumph in his voice.

Oh Fuck. I was dealing with the monkey not the organ grinder. This day has gone from bad to calamitous.

"Stop playing games Father." Nothing yet but I feel everything tense in preparation. He walks in behind the lamp. A little murmuring between master and apprentice, so quiet I cannot pick out the words. An incantation perhaps.

"'Your place is elsewhere but tell me Father Steel, what do you know of us and who have you told?" I am resisting and he knows it. The lamp goes out and all I can see apart from white-spots are two baleful glowing red eyes. They are coming closer. I cannot close my eyes. He has them in his control.

They descend towards me closer and closer. I feel cold hands on both sides of my face and a mouth covers mine. I try to scream but his kiss floods over me causing my resistance to shatter as my mind is ravaged. A hot sweaty hand fumbles with my zip and yanks out my, surprisingly, erect member. I am lost in a sea of tortuous rapture as a second mouth engulfs my cock, sucking and pumping tearing me to a climax I cannot prevent.

Sex magic is so very potent and this bastard is an expert. His tongue fills my mouth commanding my submission as his apprentice fellates me. The ecstasy overtakes me as he feeds from my memories. Spurt after of spurt filling the bastard between my legs. I am spent and barely conscious as the kiss ends. I throw myself backwards landing with a crash on the floor. In front of me, daylight creeps along the edge of the curtains. What a dodgy pattern, seventies classic obviously. I look round to see the master drink from his apprentice. I pass out, thank god.

Chapter 29

It is dark. I am cold and I have no idea where the hell I am. Sounds like I am waking up from another whisky induced bender. I haven't had one for years. No hangover just a tender ache at the back of my neck. My hands are cold and cuffed around a pipe, so I will be going nowhere anytime soon. I try to stretch my legs out and realise I am a bit stiff and sitting in a puddle, but otherwise I am whole. Waggling my fingers and toes to get some circulation to flow.

Being locked in a dark place with no recollection of how I got here worries me, more than I would let on. I shuffle myself about until I'm able to get on my knees and then stand up. Bastards have nicked my shoes I notice as the water soaks through the soles of my thin black socks. Without being a drama queen, I am uncomfortable and its unlikely to get any better. I shiver and my teeth are just this side of chattering and if I let them they would start. Like a blind dog humping a leg I try to feel in my pocket for my phone. Not there, but that's hardly a surprise. I still have my coat on, albeit a bit wet in places, so I doubt I am being left here to die.

A rumble of road traffic jerks me back to the present and I realise that I am near a road, not hidden away in the boon-docks. Maybe I can get someone to open the container. I start banging with my hands and shouting. Well it gives me something to do, I suppose. A drip just splashed on my head, I jump away in fright and fall arse over tit in the puddle. Pain races from my wrists to my brain and I squeak like a big Jessie. This can only mean that the pipe goes out through the roof. I pull myself to a more comfortable position leaning against the corrugated wall of the container. I wait, letting myself become one with my environment, letting my ears pick out anything at all that will give me a clue as to my whereabouts.

Well at least the container is stationary, and I am not headed for Africa like a load of organ boxes. We aren't rolling on down a road either, so all good on that front for now. I can hear the occasional rumble of vehicles passing but no sounds of people. Of course it could be the middle of the night. My watch has been misappropriated by the bad guys.

A loud grumbling escapes my stomach which is as empty as my pockets, so I know it must be night time. No bird sound either, so night time it is. Feeling around with my hands I try to estimate the extent of the wet patch in which I woke up. Obviously it's the man's job to lie on the wet patch. I snigger at myself. This puddle is just sufficiently annoying as to make it difficult to get a dry bit but with a stretch and lying with my arms above my head I manage to lie on a dry bit of floor. I drift off, uncomfortable, sore, wet, cold and miserable. No doubt the next time I wake up it will be even worse. That's me Polly fucking Anna.

Rumbling almost continuous in tone suggests that morning is with me. Traffic moving past at speed on the nearby busy road has brought me back to the land of the conscious. It is still dark in my prison but not the total inky blackness that I last awoke to. Some holes in the structure are letting a little light in and from above me dripping water coming down the side of the pipe. Around it a corona of light adds to how much I can see. The backs of my hands are smeared with what looks like soot. On closer inspection they are pentagrams that have been smudged by me. Shit!

Bad enough to have been taken but to have been locked in darkness and marked is a new low for me. I rub my hands clean in the water, and then scrub my face too. The black mess that covers my hands evidence of the mark that no doubt adorned my forehead. Bastards! Twice now they have worked on me, and twice I have been caught out. They are ahead of me on points but I'm not out yet. They certainly have the upper hand, and my sulphurous swearing reveals how much I am upset. I know what they are up to but have little proof and now I am trapped and at the mercy not of a dabbling bunch of sex-game playing crazies but real practitioners of dark magic. I wonder what they have taken this time? I am in over my head.

The opening and closing of the container door, filled the space with some light for a moment. Unfortunately two henchmen have arrived to make my day complete.

"Stuck your nose in once too often Priest." Snarly voice opens the show. As intimidation goes it was a feeble attempt. He's obviously not very good and must try harder.

"You dirty rat." I do my best bogey impersonation but it fails to impress as they are too far away to hear me properly. Snarly voice, thinks its fear. So he looks happy.

Of course, I should be afraid. Wakening up chained to a pipe inside, what I presume is, a container. I don't expect them to kill me, two priests in the same month from the same church. I expect a doing but little more.

"He'll talk all right. Look he's bricking himself.' A younger voice behind me added his wisdom. He seems to like the idea of my fear. He is practically chattering like a monkey.

"Wait till the master's friend gets here." Glee fills his snotty voice; triumphalist bastards. I slump against the pipe, no point in straining for now. At least I can find the master's hideout, then we'll see. Let's see how happy they are when Brotherton and his gang kick in the doors.

Evil henchmen one and two wander off down the container, their footsteps echoing loudly. Suddenly bright light covers the floor as the door to the outside swings open. Just as swiftly it is cut off and I am left in darkness, alone once more. I try to get some sort of descriptions for Brotherton. Although I will be able to identify them should our paths cross in the future. I won't need Brotherton then.

all, balding and wearing a San Francisco Forty-Niner's jacket. Should be easy to find in Scotland. After all not too many watch American football, do they. I am a Steelers man myself. So much for dumb, the shorter nondescript is obviously Dumber. I feel a giggle building inside and now I know I'm hysterical. Dumb and dumber, Jesus.

Chapter 30

It must be getting near the time; I can feel a power gathering from all around. It's like a great big elastic band tightening around my head. If I don't get out of here soon, well I don't fancy my chances. At an appointed time, something will visit me inside this box prison and that, as they say, will be that.

The bastards will pay for this, even if I have to haunt them personally. I am getting a wee bit frazzled, no way of getting myself out of here and, worse, no way to tell anyone where I am. The headlines will be 'Priest murdered and left in a container. Police appealing for witnesses.' Will they start looking for a serial killer who bludgeons priests to death? I doubt it.

My arm is aching; pain apparently spreads up from the ends. Snapping my thumb to get the cuff off seemed like a good idea at the time. Beginning to reassess that now. I tentatively touch it, and howl in agony. Fucks sake. No point in trying to move it to a better angle, it's dangling like a limp dick. The pain is excruciating, not at all like poking a bruise. More like medieval torture. At least the cuff is off and dangling from the other wrist.

A car is approaching, one of those expanding cars, you know

the ones with music so loud that all we hear is doof-doof-doof. 'Turn the fucking music off for fucks sake.' I scream. He'll never hear me otherwise. The bright LED light from his headlights is streaming through the many little holes and outlining the doors. The engine cuts off after a flourish of vroom as his no doubt just post-pubescent right foot flicks the accelerator. Thankfully the doof-doof has stopped. The light so briefly burning my eyes has been extinguished. Now I am getting the fluorescent dancing lights on my eyes, night vision well shot now.

"Help! Lemme out!" I shout and bang on the door hoping against hope that he's not one of the enemy. The metal of the handcuff making a piercing racket. I keep banging and shouting, this is my final chance; it won't be long now until my demonic visitor will arrive. My head is being squeezed, pressure building like a kettle coming to the boil.

The door mechanism is being fumbled with. I can hear two voices, one of each gender. The lights come back on and I keep banging and shouting like a big Jessie. Dear God let them hear me. I launch my body against the steel wall making as much noise as I can.

"It's padlocked, man." A muffled young man's voice reaches me from outside. He must be all of seventeen, practically a child. At least he is trying to help.

"Smash it quickly, please! Let me out!" I know I am

hysterical but it is now or never. If he takes too long it won't matter. After an eternity of throbbing pain from thumb to shoulder measured in elevated heart beats, a hammer starts to bang on the padlock. The metallic ting like the chimes of the final clock striking my doom. I can't hear what they are saying but she's giving him instructions on what and where to hit with the hammer. Domestic avoided as her advice is followed and the lock is pulled away and the lever mechanism pulled. I throw myself out screaming.

"Run!" I stagger away from my erstwhile prison followed by the two teenagers. Their faces masks of confusion yet they follow me away from the container. They know what terror looks like and decide that I might know what I am running from.

A flash of red light and the demon arrives. The smell of brimstone is overpowering. It roars a voice filled with hate and disappointment. It has been cheated of its offering. The container rocks from side to side as the Demon storms around inside. Its rage fills the night and I am so thankful that I wasn't in there to meet it. It would have been bloody and very, very quick.

"What the fuck is that?" Spotty young saviour blurts out. His snogging partner screams a high pitched, near professional scream. The brief frozen moment we shared, well and truly over. They start to back away, slowly. It seems years of Hollywood horror movies have made a resilient population of young folk who aren't unmanned at the first supernatural encounter.

"You got a phone?" I take charge. Spotty hands me a rather nice one. He is staring into the container, and disbelief fills his eyes. He looks quite comical, she has buried her face in his chest. She's sobbing a little, what a little stereotype. I dial Brotherton two rings later and I am spilling the lot. In a stream without much of a pause.

"Where are you?" Brotherton asks and I realise I have no idea. Spotty tells me loud enough that the next village have heard him. The container stops shaking, silence has filled the night. The whimpering is all that remains. The Demon has gone; I can't feel it any more. The vice that was holding my head is gone. Only the pain throbbing up my arm is left to remind me of my ordeal. That and the cold, the wet and the growling hunger in the pit of my stomach. The Cavalry are on their way. I hand the phone back to my young spotty friend.

"Thanks man. You saved my ass." Not what he expects and his eyes alight on my dog-collar. I smile back, a little wild but coming back down a bit.

"Father, was that real?" His voice almost afraid to ask. He wasn't quite ready to trust his own eyes. After all, a Demon isn't what you expect to see when out for a snog.

I nod. It's about all I can manage. I am a wreck, knees out of my trousers, handcuffs hanging from my good wrist, limp-dick thumb swelling like a sausage, black eye, split lip, covered in dust. What a picture. I think he will be converted after tonight's experience.

Brotherton arrived three car lengths in front of the marked police car. The blue flashing light illuminates the scene, casting weird shadows all around. His dismount and approach of the container are very smooth and professional. He peeks inside then moves away. I hadn't noticed how big he actually is. I would want him on my side if we are picking teams.

"It's empty." I tell him. I really should say something grateful but I don't. I am too fucked to care.

"You OK? You look like shit." I know he's happy to see me too. He points past my shoulder and does the air hostess thing to his posse of police constables. You there, you that way. All efficient and cop-like. A well oiled machine in action.

"My rescuers are in the car." I flick my head in the general direction, "You better take their statements. This needs a lid kept on it." A little widening of his eyes shows he gets my drift. He pulls his walkie-talkie from somewhere and rustles up an ambulance for me. I must really look like shit. I need a seat so Brotherton's car it is. The seats will clean. I hope.

I must have zonked out. Some new voice is calling me sir. I just let my eyes close for a minute, the headrest felt so good. The throbbing pains around my body like a lullaby just easing me to sleep.

"Can you hear me sir? Wake up." I thought they were trained not to panic but it's there at the edges of his voice. "Father Steel, can you hear me?" He is persistent at any rate.

"I'm fine. I'm fine." I surface to see a paramedic, in his natty fluorescent green and yellow uniform, squatting in the open car door space. His face showing a concern I hadn't really expected over a broken thumb.

"It's my thumb." I don't move my arm towards him. After everything, I tell him it's my thumb. Perhaps I am not fine after all. Maybe I have had a blow to the head.

"That's the least of our problems, I think." He smiles as he looks into my eyes. "We are going to need to go to the hospital. We need to get you checked out." He signals his partner and speaks into his microphone thing. Do they all ave them these days? I want one next time, then I would be able to call my own cavalry.

"Let's get you over to the ambulance, can you manage that?" Like policemen, ambulance men are getting younger these days. I shuffle my ass out of Brotherton's car and stand up, I am suddenly light headed but he has a hold of my good arm and I womble over to the ambulance. Apparently adrenalin had gotten me this far and I am now utterly wiped. My legs are like spaghetti and remind me of Bruce Grobbelaar and that penalty.

The place is swarming with policemen, yellow tape rings the scene and there is no sign of spotty and the girl. Don't see Brotherton either. The haven of the ambulance is close and in a few moments I am introduced to Steve and John, my paramedic crew. They are very thorough, checking all the easy things and lying me down. I notice a mood change as I start to struggle to focus. My lip is blue apparently and we are off. The trolley thing feels very comfortable, and my eyelids are so heavy. Fuck it I give in. Lights out. Steve keeps speaking to me.

Chapter 31

Having been somewhat busy for the last day or two, sitting in a none-too-comfortable hospital bed, one tends to be out of the loop. A loop that the bad guys are well and truly wired into. When I turned out not to be demon dinner, someone had to be, it seems. Being apprentice to a Dark Master can be a hazardous career choice. There, on the front page of the local rag, was the apprentice that had eluded me at the civic reception.

"Council Leader's special advisor found dead in Riverside Park" was the big black headline. Reading further words like unexplained and suspicious litter, what can only be called, pretty piss poor, copy. Add journalists to the list of getting younger these days. The story was littered with poorly constructed sentences and inaccuracies.

"I know why he is expired." I say out loud. Talking to myself is an age old habit. I wonder what Brotherton knows about it. Body was found bobbing in the River Leven, inside the park. It had been there a couple of days, so the press have informed me.

"Yer Arse." I know when he died almost to the minute. So

my experience in the container reminds me. My ribs hurt and my red raw wrists, covered by pretty little white bandages, are reminders of a rather close call. The panda look is not my best one, a suspected broken nose and split lip very visual reminders to everyone else that I had suffered a mishap. A fall I am telling anyone who looks gullible enough to believe me. A doing would be the professional commentary.

So my enemy works through a proxy or medium, is cautious and, most definitely, not a fool. Summonings are a risky business. Calling forth a powerful, supernatural, extra-planar being requires sacrifice and iron control. Any loss of control and a life is paid. My adversary has lost a well placed tool. The game is turning and turning in my favour at last. Of course if this is winning then thank God we aren't losing.

"Brotherton." He answers on the second ring; I am impressed. He's giving nothing away. I hope he can talk.

"Steel. I see we have a new body." No point pissing about. I want to know what the inside track is.

"We? It's related?" He needs to ask? He is definitely in need of some Padawan training. Of course it is related.

"Yes." That's me, expansive as hell. What a poker player eh? I want to get him really focussed and not distracted by little mundanities like facts.

"In what way? There's no connection. Looks like it could be

a drug overdose or something unexplained." Oh dear, he's backsliding. I had such high hopes for him too. I sigh, a little too loudly and Brotherton pauses feeling the sting of my disappointment. Or at least I imagine he does.

"He was the apprentice to the Dark Master." I pause, suspense and all that. "I felt him at the civic reception the other week. I recognise his face." Smug smart arse is kicking in now. I have been lying around for a few days after all.

"Right, well we'd better have a chat about this." Brotherton has obviously remembered where he is and is not willing to have this chat here.

"Brotherton, this poor sod took my place and was sacrificed to feed the Demon. The Demon that was summoned to kill me. A poor trusting fool, betrayed by his master. We are starting to win.' Okay winning was a bit optimistic but he needed a pick-me-up.

"The Post Mortem will be back later today. We'll get a cause of death then." All professional cop-like again. I am so disappointed.

"I'll bet on a rare cancer causing heart failure, undiagnosed obviously." I might as well strut. If only I could do lottery numbers.

"Rest up and I'll swing by later with the report." Oh he does care. The line goes dead. He doesn't care that much, apparently.

Seeing as I am stuck in my utilitarian lodge room, convalescing, I suppose I should give some thought to solving this case. The Bishop expects me to, after all.

"What do we know?'" I muse out loud. This won't really take long but it will pass the time and there is no way I am watching Jeremy-bloody-Kyle. Daytime television is a buffet of mental programmes and chat shows with as many unrepresentative people as can be crammed in. Whatever happened to Richard and Judy?

"MacPhail killed by a summoned demon. Why? No idea." This might be really quick; it appears I know the square root of eff all. I can't actually answer the why of the key question. Motive escapes me, totally.

"Cult in St Margaret's and organ trafficking in Africa." I suck as a detective, usually cases are attrition with a serendipitous ending. Called dumb luck, if the truth be told. I can trace organs and shipping; which is a start. I know there is a cult and a satanic disciple, expired, and a Dark Master. What is irritating is that I can't tie these together in a coherent narrative with evidence. I was kidnapped after all. Surely there is something. I can probably find the house too.

"One funds the other but why kill MacPhail? I can't see him as a willing sacrifice." My head is empty and my bladder full, so I painfully wince my way to the loo. I get a fright as the fluorescent lighting does me no favours.

"Why would you off one of your own guys?" I look in the mirror as I aim my bits. It is truly amazing where inspiration strikes.

"MacPhail wasn't a team player! What if he had gone native? Wanted to come out or seize power for himself?" I think I am on to something, and hopefully not a painkiller fuelled delusion. It might be part of the picture. They might not have been one happy family.

"A power struggle in their little cult of sex maniacs? Why not something basic?" It was getting juicier by the second and, like all fantastic theories of mine, not a fact to corroborate it in sight. Evidence? Who needs that? Let's just roll with it for now.

I flop back onto my bed, replaying and rethinking what I know through my new prism. So if MacPhail was a challenge to the Master, then what? It's not like they would get a ready made replacement from the Diocese. Can't exactly advertise, can they? 'Satanic Priest required for cult in new town.' I wonder if their reach is great enough to get a priest of their choice? Then I recall the selection committee that actually picks the priest is made from the locals. They approve the candidate they want. It would be a closed loop, perpetually placing their man in the manse.

"It's about the money!" I say it like it's a fact. I amaze myself, really. Was MacPhail greedy? Did he want a bigger cut?

I'll bet the fucker did, or perhaps he had had enough. You know, got bored of the sex and power. Perhaps he wanted to retire with pockets of dosh to a warmer, happier, climate. Maybe, just maybe, it was good old fashioned greed. Perhaps he threatened to expose the operation and became a liability? Doubtful, but you never know. I can't wait to run my thinking past Brotherton. I can almost see his serious cop face 'Where's the proof?' Bollocks.

"Apparently he had a cardiac arrest while using the outdoor gym, trim-trail thing. Died and then fell into the river. It was brought on by an underlying, very rare and undiagnosed, condition." Brotherton was trying his best not to be sour. I knew he was trying though.

"Cancer was it?" I am unbearable, sometimes. That superior facial expression settling into place, I don't even practice. I am a natural. A bit like the crowing of Peter Pan.

"Apparently so, a very rare one in five hundred thousand kind of cancer that's almost impossible to detect." He knows I am going to gloat.

"He shoots…He scores!" The basketball air shot meeting my commentary. Juvenile but I can't help myself. They are hardly going to put the cause of death as 'Soul extracted by aggravated encounter with a Demon' are they? Although the millennium has passed so who knows.

"Amazing how mundane demon induced deaths can be made to sound. Anyone see the myocardial-infarction?'" I pause, eyebrow cocked "I'll bet not. How long until he was discovered and by whom? Do they think us that stupid? How far did he need to stagger to throw himself in the river?"

Brotherton looks perturbed. He knows I am right but the case is closed. The body of our enemy discovered but no case to follow up. He looks at me, expectantly. What he expects I have no idea.

Chapter 32

I should get a frequent visitor award or a badge or something. I have been in the Bishop's residence more times in the last month than in the last year. I wonder if there is such a thing? Perhaps air miles could be awarded. I park next to the dark blue Volvo, not round the back as the doorman continually reminds me to do. I do it just to wind him up, and it does. Contrary, that's me. I crunch my way across the gravel giving the door time to open, and sure enough it does, just as I mount the first step. The step looks worn from the many feet that have passed this way and not one of them with a frequent visitor award; nor a card.

"Welcome Father." He puts out a hand for my coat. His resistance to being a doorman has been eroded and his acceptance is complete. I smile as I hand it over. "The Bishop is in the study," He knows I know where it is. "You are to go on through." He hides his disapproval very well these days, or maybe he likes me now. Not very likely, though.

In moments I am sitting in the corner of a red leather Chesterfield sofa looking at His Eminence over his oversize desk. Surely he isn't compensating. He waves me over to a coffee pot as he reads some official looking papers. He mumbled something about Jeremy, I am presuming it isn't Jeremy Kyle, so I will wait and be mother when Father Jeremy gets here.

It is a lovely study. French doors letting in floods of light from the terrace, fading the curtains, carpet and couches equally, creates a lovely ambiance. A wall of bookshelves, with many very old and unread tomes, stand along one wall and the fireplace with its large mirror above it covers the other. A smattering of religious art fills in the wall gaps. It should feel cluttered but it doesn't. Even I could work in here. Well more likely I would get distracted by the texts of the ancients and lose all track of time. His computer looks a bit out of place but don't they always. I wonder how much of this room is hand-me-down and how much is his aesthetic. I'm betting it has pretty much looked like this for ages. The wooden shelves and panels have that old, cared for, look and if there wasn't a bloody air freshener thingy I would be able to smell them. No nasty brown staining from cigarettes in here, I don't think anyone would dare.

Bishop Michael's brow is furrowing as he dislikes what he's reading. His lips narrow in disapproval completing the wasp chewing expression. I hope it's not about me. It looks as if I am about to find out as the reading glasses are removed with a weary sigh. He looks into his coffee cup and delivers another weighty sigh, finding it empty. The study door opens and Father Jeremy bustles in. He approaches, genuflects and kisses the Bishop's ring, which I neglected to do. What a suck up.

"Bishop Michael, Andrew. We have much to discuss." Like he knows something very important. His man bag looks full to bursting, so no doubt he will pull something out of it.

"Father Jeremy, please be seated." The Bishop has great manners. I just nod, thankful to have avoided a pre-meeting scolding. I am such a let down, obviously. I rise like a pregnant cow from the couch and venture to the coffee pot, delaying the inevitable. I probably can't be civil without the caffeine.

"Coffee anyone?" I try to sound upbeat, positive maybe. Nods greet me and the Bishop extends his empty cup towards me. I'd better fill it then. I'd better not drip on his desk either.

"The Sabbat is nearing." Melodramatic opening from Father Jeremy. I resist my usual snide replies. "And we are no nearer to knowing where it will take place." He looks worried that we'll miss it. Like buses I am sure there will be another one once the apocalyptic disaster has passed.

"Nothing yet." I intone. It is my failure, obviously. Bishop Michael frowns again. He picks up the paper he was reading. He waves it about, showing it has an imposing logo on it, Home Office apparently. Oh dear I am failing on a whole new level.

"The Home Secretary isn't exactly pleased with our progress on this one. It seems the press have gotten a sniff of something and needed warding off." Oh no, the press. Run. I keep that one inside, too.

"They have some lurid pictures of your abuse Andrew. Full colour, news of the world stuff. A total bloody mess." Disgust written large across his face, not directed at me I hope. I didn't actually agree to it, as I am sure he knows.

"I haven't seen them." Probably not helping with that one. I put on my neutral face. Blame the victim for getting worked over and being used.

"They are very explicit, do you want them for a scrap book?" I decide that one is rhetorical and decline to answer. No piccies will be forthcoming then. Although I might have been able to identify some of them in the future.

"We need this lot wrapped up quickly. Jeremy what have you gleaned from the book Andrew recovered?" The focus of his ire has swung away from me, thankfully. Father Jeremy needs to deliver or he will get 'the face'.

"It's a genuine Grimoire with details of rituals and the like. It matches with some of our reference texts. Some very detailed and downright depraved. How many have been performed, it is impossible to tell." Jeremy pauses for a sip of, frankly disgusting over-brewed, coffee before continuing. "Their calendar of Sabbats is consistent with ones we know already which worries me. This coming weekend they have a High Mass and can open the portal." He looks anxious. What is he not telling us?

"Without the Book will they be able to perform the ritual?" Bishop Michael looking for a crumb of comfort throws it out there. He needs some good news to relay to the Home Secretary; I have the feeling there won't be any.

"I believe their Master will have his own copy." Jeremy's face looks like he has finally tasted the coffee. "Midnight on Sunday and the Gate will be opened, letting something through."

"If we interrupt their ritual, will it stop the Portal being opened?" I hear my own voice sounding reasonable. Perhaps fervently hopeful would be a better description.

"I don't know. Maybe, maybe not. The details on the Portal are very vague. It may not be contingent on the ritual. Perhaps all it needs is the sacrifice." Jezza confirms my worst fears. We might not stop them. Demon running amok, we are all doomed. Doomed I tell you.

"Andrew, we need the venue. The earlier the better. I will brief the Home Secretary, and he won't be pleased." He swigs his coffee which, going by his face, has cooled. It was bad enough when it was hot. Mine is largely untouched.

My phone rings, probably should have put it to silent. Oh dear. I make the excuse face and leave into the panelled hallway glad to be out of there in one piece.

Chapter 33

I know my life is like the Indiana Jones meets the exorcist but a whole host of proper priestly stuff needs to be done. I need to maintain the orderly running of the parish while I root out the bastards that have kidnapped and worked me over. Let alone the vengeance that is to be visited upon them for the sexual liberties they have taken with me. The congregation don't all know about the war being waged on their turf or rather on God's turf. This little family's problems must not be aired in public.

So far I have managed not to get back into Angela Brookes bed, she and I both need a break. Me to recover from the physical damages I have sustained and she to recover from the ordeal of being abducted and being unable to speak about it. I have answered her texts; I am not that cold but there has been little playfulness in them. I am hoping that the cleansing and confessional undertakings I gave can be maintained. It will be easier if I don't get in the same room as her too soon. Her vulnerable look was heartbreaking, last time we met. It was public so there was no physical contact either. I had struggled not to hold her and protect her in my arms. I had managed that at least.

Anyway, surrounded by a pile of utterly pointless paperwork, I am ensconced in the cramped little office, that serves the church building. A gentle knock at the door generates the automatic reply "Come in." The door opens quietly and I am surprised to see the rather pretty daughter of my erstwhile paramour. She is very pretty and looking very serious. She has the echo of her mother in her features and probably why she seems so much older than her tender years.

"Father." She does innocence, fatally well. I know now why so many men are burning in hell for thoughts that they had been unable to avoid.

"Michelle, how lovely to see you." Warning bells going off all over the place, danger. What was she doing here? She is dressed to get a reaction. Short skirt and satin blouse package her very obvious assets. She knows it too, having used this approach before I expect. Or perhaps seen it used by her mother.

"I came to see you, Father. I need your help." She seemed uncertain, and a little concerned. I waited. Let's see where this was going. What did she know? Worse still I was probably being set up again. Her lip being gripped between her white, flawless teeth. I bet years of braces were needed as a child and the pay-off is plain to see.

"It's about the celebration here on Sunday night. I don't want to mess up." Here we go, information about to fall in my lap. Either that or another trap. How deep is she in? I'm in over my head so no doubt she is too.

"In what way, Michelle?" Keep it simple and don't push. Festinare lente, as my old Latin teacher would have said. Hurry slowly it had meant and he used it about running in the corridor but it fit well here.

"I haven't, you know, done IT before." She managed to get it out. She was a virgin and she was involved or was about to be. Her cheeks had taken on a flush that put truth to her lie of seductive vixen. She was exactly what she was a girl on the brink of womanhood and subject to the worries that everyone has as they transition.

"I see.'" I try not to faint. Apparently there had been no need to lock her up in a tower to protect her from boys. Good girl. She had been very grown up about her body then. I found that sadly reassuring that her virginity was intact and she was involved with a satanic cult.

"Mum says that I should speak to you." I try not to choke as I drink my lukewarm coffee. Angela sent me her daughter to deflower? I doubt it. Was this an opening? Surely she knew what it would mean. Angela must know that I am here to break the cult and that would involve trouble for members.

"She says that you are the best person to resolve my

problem." Michelle had taken her mother's comments to mean that I should be her first. The look on her young face was one I never wanted to see again. Functional lust; wanting it done in a business-like way. Did she expect me to do her here? Now?

There it was. Coded and delivered in such a way as to get Angela and Michelle out of the mess they are in. Michelle perhaps has no idea of just how deep a mess it is. The child thinks that it is all a sexy, grown up thing with no threat to her mortal soul.

"I guess I am." I try to sound normal about it, "What else did your mother say?" I need to make sure that everything works out right. I need to make sure there is no misunderstanding that screws us all. For once I want to reduce the collateral damage and devastation that will occur if the Brookes family is exposed in the press or courts. David Brookes is a decent guy whose only crime is not seeing what was going on in his household.

"That Sunday night was a big event and people from all over would be here. I would need to be ready for my turn on the altar." She didn't seem too phased about that, apparently. Her acceptance seemed total. Was I too late? It sounded like she was discussing doing maths homework or prepping for an exam. The pain in my chest sharp and immediate, she so needed saving and I was probably years late to start the job.

"Has your mother told you what happens?" I try to see just

what has been explained, and perhaps glean some insights. Hopefully I could shock her out of this and keep her safe. Probably a forlorn hope but I would have to try.

"Oh yes. The ritual sacrifice is there for all too see, touch and use." The last bit was a bit too enthusiastic. A gleam of something is in her eyes. A lust for something she hadn't yet had and that no one so young should have to experience.

"It sounds simple, doesn't it?" I keep my voice bland but want to scream Noooo! I try to pull her eyes to mine, away from the spot above my head that her eyes have found so interesting.

"I can do it. It's not like I haven't seen our local mass." Oh dear, innocence well and truly lost. She seems to be ready to step up, like a new player on the roster. Fresh meat for the fat, lumpy swingers club of the satanic coven. What a total sin to have embroiled her in this already. I wondered who to be more angry at; MacPhail or Angela Brookes?

"Local meetings are less imposing for a young girl like you. After all you know all the people, don't you?" I try to curb her zeal. I want her to think about the less than perfect people who will have their mouths and paws all over her body; not to mention the other appendages.

"Father, that's part of the problem. I don't want Mr Reid to be my first and he has been leering at me for ages. He's gross." Her distaste curls her lip. Not that I blame her, he must have been one of the fatter, wobblier celebrants last time. She has standards after all.

"You do not choose who takes you on the altar." I sound stern, but really I am terrified for her. She bows her head quickly. I need to stay in my role or we are all in the shit.

"I am sorry, Master.'" She says so softly. Master! Oh dear Lord this isn't happening. I must prevent her ultimate corruption if nothing else. I wonder if she is confirmed in their faith or if they have a different process.

"Michelle, Being on the altar is a great honour and not one given lightly." I pause; her head is still bowed so I have no idea what she is thinking. I wonder if I can simply say she isn't ready this time?

"Teach me Master, make me ready." Fervour fills her shiny, beautiful eyes. She would be irresistible had I been MacPhail; perhaps he had been saving her for a special occasion.

"Has your mother not told you what to do and how to do it?" I try for a disapproving stance. Like all mothers teach their daughters how to be a sacrificial fuck at a Sabbat. After all what skills does one mother pass on to the next generation?

"I know how to, you know, with my mouth." She says it like it is so ordinary. "But what if it hurts too much the first time? I don't want to be a failure and mum has told me that some can be quite big and rough."

I stare at her, trying for aloof not shocked into insensibility. "Yes they can. Did your mother tell you about the women too?" Let's try for another shock attack, might just put her off. Although that is looking so remote at this point.

"That will be okay, Hannah and I sometimes practice on each other and I don't mind." I try not to faint. Bloody hell, Hannah too. Which one was Hannah?

"I see. Then all you need is a practice or two before Sunday?" I make it sound ordinary. Lose cherry, get ready for orgy within the week. Almost like a to do list that hangs on the fridge door. You know; get milk, put bins out, lose virginity for gang bang.

"That's why I am here." She stands up and begins unbuttoning her blouse. Her flawless young skin exposed with each button. What a lovely white lace bra too.

"Stop." I raise my hand. "I will not rush this for you. We will do it properly but not here and not now. I have others to attend to." Whoa, Time out. Run screaming from the room before I have a seizure and give the game away.

Looking confused and, luckily she isn't feeling spurned, uncertain she waits. She starts to re-button. I think I see tears forming at the edges of her very pretty eyes. Better that she is upset now than the alternatives. I smile paternally to her, hoping to lessen the blow.

"Michelle, you are young and very beautiful. You deserve a

very special initiation and not be squandered under the less than worthy hands of the Mr Reids of this world." I lift her chin gently, making sure her eyes meet mine "When you are finally laid out on the altar, you will be magnificent." I pray she is buying in to this. I kiss her on the forehead and send her on her way, lucky to have escaped this mess without imperilling my mortal soul. How to stall her for the next few days and keep her out of my bed might be a bit trickier.

More importantly I have the time and place of their Grand Sabbat. Father Jeremy will be deliriously happy. This will give us a chance to smash this ring of organ trafficking Satanists and more than that save Angela Brookes and her innocent daughter from the depravities that might lie in store for them. Innocent being a relative term, obviously.

"Brotherton." I speak quietly into my phone. No point in taking chances. "I have a real breakthrough. I know where and when. There is a little fly in my ointment, however."

"Excellent. We need to talk. You can tell me about your ointment problem." He has learned so much from our association. I am almost proud of him.

"Costa, twenty minutes. See you there." And we are back in the game.

Chapter 34

I always thought the police squad room thing was just Hill Street Blues fantasy but now I know better. In what looks like a modern lecture theatre, at Fife's finest Police HQ, the backchat and chatter is flowing. The personalities are a right mixture with jokers and pokers in equal mix. They do look a bit young though. I see the local inspector standing, all smartly uniformed, to one side. He looks anxious; he is one of only a handful of people who know what is going down tonight. Beside him, Brotherton stands all ready to go. His blue eyes standing bright under the lights. There has been a total silence on this operation and that is how it will stay. I scan the room looking to see if there are traitors in our midst. Unless the cop that kneed me in the nuts is here, my search will come up empty.

"All right people, knock it off." The inspector raises his voice and the room stills. I can't recall his name, I think it was Sunderson. Of course it might have been Sanderson but his accent was tricky. Some dialects of Scots tongue are indecipherable.

"All radios to be deposited in the inspection tray that is

coming round. All mobile phones to go in, too." A buzz permeates the group, they know there is a big thing going down. All happy faces they are not. You would think that we had cut a few hands off. After all how can we manage for a few hours without texting or Facebook.

"Inspector Brotherton has command for this operation. This is operation porcupine. Over to you Brotherton." Sunderson moves away from the podium, he looks like a competent beat cop who has seen it all. The hubbub of noise is as expected after the choice of operation name; something about a bunch of pricks wafts across the room. The tittering and suppressed laughter follows. Like all uniformed services the banter can be a bit puerile.

"Good evening. For those of you who don't know me I am Inspector Brotherton, CID. I have been put in command of tonight's operation and we will be leaving soon to get into position. There is a comms blackout on this one so no-one and I repeat no-one will have any contact outside until after the conclusion of this operation." He paused and stared round the room, daring any comment. A pin dropping would have been heard. The phones and radios were moved to the front. Brotherton felt safe to continue. His serious mien transmitting across the faces looking back at him.

"Tonight we are going to raid a paedophile ring." The words

fell like thunder on the room. This was what they had trained for. All humour evaporated and they were ready. I didn't want him using the words Satanic Cult, so paedophiles was the way we would describe it. If they violated Hannah they would be. Funny how crimes against children get men so angry; especially as most paedophiles are men. I wondered at the tension building in the room, how many of them have kids of their own?

"We will be securing a stand alone building in the Gleninch area, and will proceed only on receipt of a go order. There will be armed response officers standing by but I hope we will not require them." Brotherton, is actually very good at this. I was even listening to his orders.

"We want to ensure we gather up as many of them as we can so there will be a Transit per two officers. The processing will take place tonight in the main hall. There is a complete black out on this until the Home Office say otherwise. Nothing will be entered into your notebooks, all records will be taken at processing in the hall."

A hand went up, about half way back. Here comes the trouble. I could see the back of his head but not his face. There is always one in any crowd, like a heckler at a comedian.

"Will we have video deployed as we make the raid?" A dark haired constable projects his voice across the whole room. A sensible question, I suppose. Good for that tricky evidence thing.

Brotherton smiles, obviously ahead of that curve. Looking at the officer who asked. He obviously knows him and likes the man.

"Stills and video will be taken as the raid progresses. We will want to identify as many as possible should the net be less tight than we hope." His voice covering the details, no notes or aids.

"We will be leaving in 10 minutes to our muster point. Any more questions?" considering Brotherton has told them very little, they have no questions. The pairings are read out. A few jokes and groans are the response. Drivers are given keys. The officers move about finding their partners for the operation.

Brotherton steps away from the podium.

Brotherton, Sunderson and I are in a squad car, no transit van for us. As only Brotherton and I know where we are going, we are in front of a cavalcade of ten transit vans. No flashing lights, no sirens, nothing. An anti climax if ever there was one. I suppose it is better if we have the element of surprise. Inspector Sunderson looks less than pleased that he has no idea where we are going. I pulled a Home Office Carte Blanche and that was it really. He hasn't addressed me directly since he phoned to check my credentials. I think he might be in the huff. I think he is too old for that sort of thing but I have had my moments too.

The plan is that I get dropped off, sneak in to the church, witness the defiling of virgins and call in the cavalry. Simple really. What a plan. I would like to claim credit for it. That might explain why it will be a disaster, if my churning guts are anything to go by.

It is nearing Eleven o'clock about an hour until the main event. Where are we going to hide the fleet of white vans? We aren't. Brotherton is going to have them drive to a different area and wait. Less chance of a leak or any late comers noticing a congregation of coppers. He must have pulled cops from all over to get this many in one place; budgets have reduced the numbers of bobbies on the beat in recent years. No matter what the politicians tell us.

It's my stop and Brotherton makes me check that my phone is charged and primed. We give it a dry run. The bleep emanating from Brotherton's device means text received. All good then. I am deposited on the pavement a few streets over from the target. The circus drives away, leaving me to go on alone. It is bloody freezing and I put up my collar, that's me cooler than Elvis. Hopefully I can avoid ending up dead and meeting him in person. God is a big Elvis fan, I believe. After all, who isn't?

The clicking of my footsteps on the cracked paving stones sounds like a parade approaching and guaranteed to give me away. The incessant need to look over my shoulder in the gaps between the orange fluorescent street lights is getting a bit old already. Apparently I am nervous. Wow, who knew?

Chapter 35

Superninja, that's me. It seemed a great idea at the time. After my last foray into St Margaret in the fields after dark went so well, you'd think I might have been a bit more circumspect. Apparently not. When Brotherton said that we need eyes on the event before we storm in, I should have kept my mouth firmly shut. Instead I heard my voice saying 'I will go.' Bizarrely no one tried to stop me. Sneaking into a black mass without an invite was beyond any level of lunacy to which I had ever descended.

Yet here I was, softly turning the back door handle (again) and expecting to sneakily infiltrate. Seriously? You couldn't make it up. There were no cars in the car park, so maybe we have the wrong venue for tonight's events. I'm not sure if I want that to be true. The consequences of this being the wrong place don't really bear thinking about. Mind you, they are hardly going to turn up en masse and fill the car park. Perhaps the curtain twitchers would notice that sort of thing.

However, the discrete path to the back door would be the way I would expect most of them to use. I have a quick look over my shoulder, you know that moment where you realise that you might get caught. Tonight, in about twenty seconds, there would be a power cut in this sector of Gleninch. A lights out to create a dark cushion to allow the forces of law and order approach without being seen. Nothing suspicious in that. The last power cuts in the town were during the seventies and the three day week. Do you think the Cult, preparing for their Highest Sabbat and event in Millennia might get suspicious? Of course not.

Power and lights out in ten, nine, eight. Or not, they are out now. Slow watch or excitable electrician? Who knows? Premature de-illumination. I enter quickly and restore the door and the curtain. Four steps later I am in the vestry office. I close the door behind me to a tiny crack. Just in time too, as two big beefy blokes move quickly to double lock and bolt the back door. Correct venue and they are too late. After a few moments checking the door and the kitchen they move off again, I continue my silent hyperventilating and perspiring session. I'll give it a minute. I have a 'GO' text ready on my phone. One button press is all it will take to get the message to the cavalry, all eventualities covered, I hope.

I can hear a low chant coming down the carpeted halls, a procession of sorts, I expect. It is in Latin, of course. Bloody copycats. My hair stands on end as they enter the church and the closing of the doors mutes their devotions. They have begun. I peek through the crack before venturing out of my haven. No one about. Quickly I unlock and unbolt the double-locked back door. Escape route or entry for reinforcements secured I make my way along to watch the show, and what a show it is.

From my vantage point, coming in behind the organ, I have an unobstructed view of their service. They are all robed and masked: the pale phantom of the opera kind not the rubber ex-president Nixon kind. The church has had a similar make-over to the last time but this time there must be fifty of them filling the pews. This is no coven but a gathering of coven. There seems to be a hierarchy with some in Red robes and not the standard black. It is one of these Red Robes that steps forward and begins.

His robe parts and flaps exposing pale flesh underneath, but not in an overtly exhibitionistic way. Just a by product of movement. I wonder what the view looks like from his side; the gaping robes exposing many breasts of which I can see the covered backs. It is like a restricted view ticket at the football; a bloody pillar in the way of the action.

"Tonight is a great night. We will celebrate the joys of our master. Our lusts shall be his, his lust shall be our sustenance and his power will flow into us. Do you hear Him?" He intones, his head bowing. He is a tall man, and the robe hangs dramatically on his long, lean frame. A glimpse inside reveals scraggly hair covering his chest.

"We hear." And they bow theirs in response. All very religious; sadly not mine. The responses are all well known and that doesn't bode well for the reach of these bastards.

"Tonight we shall share two delicate flowers. Two souls freed from the Nazarene, two bodies to fill with our secret powers. Two spirits to set free." His gaze moves to the far wall and I see two white-robed, slim forms kneeling with their heads bowed. A picture of demure subservience. I know who they are. 'They are the instruments of your doom matey.' I smile grimly, at that thought. You will be spending the rest of your days in Peterhead sex offenders wing. Sharing a cell with Big Bubba.

"Tonight Our Master will join us. Tonight, this High Sabbat, our sacrifices will be rewarded. Tonight the Void will open and we shall be filled. In our sacrament we shall hear His voice, His words and His will. We shall obey." His sermon voice fills the room. Nothing mystical happening yet. I have the host in both pockets, Holy water, Holy Unction, salt, crucifix- you know the essentials. So far so good. Can't call in the cavalry yet; no one has committed a crime. Well a crime against God, but he will take care of that in due course.

His arms outstretched in supplication, head thrown back, his Red robe parts exposes his stiffening member. A bell tinkles its pure tones in the church and from the front row a black robe ascends the two steps and kneels before him. The ankles look female and the bobbing of her head evidence of her action and role. I can feel the pressure build as they begin their offering. After a few moments she mounts the altar, her nakedness complete as her robe is untied. She must be the starter.

I hope I can avoid passing out before they commit the acts we will prosecute. I have seen this show before so it is much less interesting to me. However, it seems that due to numbers, impromptu sideshows have commenced. A veritable sex-fuelled getting to know you session. So this is how they Pax Vobiscum, it will never catch on. The red guys seem to be the busiest. Or rather they seem to be the busiest recipients. I keep my eyes peeled that neither Hannah nor Michelle are included. They are kneeling demurely, forgotten almost. Like pure little statues, untouched and unseen.

The circling of the altar and partaking of the offering goes on apace but somehow tonight feels different. There is very little build up of mystical pressure, it seems to dissipate as soon as it is generated. Almost like the valve has been left open preventing any pressure building up. Odd. I would think that they'd need it to build to a climax to open the portal. The pressure I felt making my ears pop has been replaced by a low thrum. This is amateur level of dabbling, although I know they are serious. I wait. I am a little uncertain; I have cavalry to call and nothing but a swingfest to report.

You've got to admire Red Robe's restraint. He has been sliding in and out of her throat for about ten minutes while the sideshows have all come to a peak; casting their seed and convulsing through paroxysms of pleasure. They are drawing breath before the entrée. He withdraws himself as his partner descends the altar, smiling and apparently honoured. Another chime of the bell. Its game time.

He turns his masked face to the white-robed and hooded pair. His index finger points and they stand. They look a little wooden as they move forward to the rail. Their robes, I notice, are of a very different design and very, very flimsy. They drape beautifully, skimming their delicate forms. Their arousal, or chill, very evident.

"Do you freely consent to giving this night?" His sermon voice reaching all corners of the church. I am sure he thinks that is a disclaimer that will keep him out of the deepest shit. Like hell it will.

"I do." They chime together, almost mono-tonal. I can tell them apart but I wonder if this consent, freely given, will be sufficient cover for these bastards. The law sometimes lets us all down.

"Then come, make your offering to the night. Make a gift of your bodies and feed our Horned Master. His gift of rapture is yours to receive and enjoy." His happy member bobs in anticipation as he waves them forward. I wonder which will be first. Hannah apparently, her face coming into view under the candlelight. She steps slowly up the steps as two black cloaked hand maidens rip the robe from her. The violent tearing sound is like a thunderclap in the silence. All eyes are focussed hard on her, now naked, body. Which from the rear is, no doubt, whetting a few, very undesirable, appetites in the audience.

"Make your offering." The command is clear – perform. She knows her role. Who has been priming her I do not know but she doesn't hesitate.

I press my one button and call for reinforcements is sent. Hannah on all fours presents to the room; she will be taken by those present. Faceless strangers who will enjoy her body as she supplicates the master before her. I am so not allowing this. I know its not the plan but too bad. Brotherton will just need to catch up.

"By all that's Holy, stop!" My voice is loud and full of reach. I call it my fear of god voice. Collective whiplash strikes the gathered Faithful. "This abomination is over." I stride from the shadows like an avenger. What now? I have no idea, stalling time. I sometimes wish I had a sword to draw like Michael.

I expect a running for the door type stampede as they are discovered but they are rather calm. Perhaps a few erections have drooped but not quite the response I was expecting. I might be in trouble.

"Take him." A contemptuous command as he returns his attention to Hannah. Four large habit-wearing heavies close in on me. Oh shit, time to make like a rabbit and try to evade them. It is a futile effort as their outstretched hands grab and pull at me. My hay-maker of a right hook connects with a cheek shattering the mask and causing excruciating pain to shoot up my arm. I recognise the nuts-kneeing traffic cop, who was so kind to me last time. He doesn't look too amused. My nuts ache at the impending reunion with his knee. I am now effectively smothered and held on the ground as he exacts retribution for my punch. His stamp on my crotch ends all resistance. I am rolled into the side as the show goes on.

Violence and sex are a powerful cocktail and I feel the band of pressure build around my head, squeezing my skull. I can see through my tears that Hannah is an athletic and willing participant. Her back is smattered with shining libations delivered by an enthusiastic front row. A virgin she most certainly was not. Dear God, Brotherton, hurry the fuck up.

"Enjoy the show, Worm." One of the gang of four smirks. I stare at his plastic covered face, knowing that I will be getting the last laugh.

"Fuck you." I manage to get out. My lungs are really not getting much to work with. The stars that twinkle around the edges of my vision tell me that oxygen might be in a bit of a short supply.

"Oh they will, just like last time. Your turn will come." His triumphant leer needs wiped off his smarmy face. I clench my eyes shut but the very vocal encouragement and pornographic soundtrack fill my ears. A guttural roar of release causes the room to quieten and all the sexual energy to dissipate. I see her raised to her feet, used and smiling. A cloak and hood of deepest black is placed around her shoulders. One more that needs saving. Those stains will take some getting out.

"The time draws nigh." They move into a close huddle near the communion rail. Kneeling, half exposed and faces upturned, as their celebrant walks along in front of them. Their kisses on his, now coated, stiffening member are well received. Their chanting is much more serious now. Its in pigeon Latin and full of the usual mumbo jumbo. Perhaps this is the start of Father Jeremy's portal spell. I can't feel the power, its like trying to hold fog. It is disappearing as soon as it comes into being.

"Master come among us." Is their chant, repeated over and over. It is a dull monotonous and unimaginative chant but there is something not happening.

"Tonight he will come among us." Red Robe exults, his eyes shining brightly. He casts his gaze across the assembly, his face exultant. His eyes alight on the only one in white in the gathering. "Come to me child." He points and a fully compliant Michelle Brookes picks her way forward. I struggle, although I know it is futile. The foot pressing my head against the floor gives me a shunt, making tears blur my vision. For once I am glad I can't see.

Is her offering going to be enough to open the portal? I doubt it, even though she is a virgin. The power just isn't here to deliver. Fuck, blood and sex. Is she to be sacrificed? Has she been kept for a real sacrifice? A real blood opening of the portal?

"Watch Maggot, and savour your failure." Where do they get their lines? Is there a book of sinister and lame Satanist phrases? A satanic phrases for dummies? Hammer House of Horror circa nineteen seventy? Michelle Brookes is lying on the Altar, passive but still clothed. The Red Robed Priest is offering a libation to those present. I shudder to think what is in that chalice but the recipients seem keen to partake. I can feel my tongue curling at the thought.

He returns to the altar his robes hiding Michelle from sight like Dracula in the movies. When he steps away blood covers her chest in a crimson pool. "Oh dear God no." I whisper, He has stabbed her. Our failure is total. She is lost and I can do nothing about it.

"Behold our sacrifice." He holds his bloody hands high. "With my blood she is marked for our master." A cut across one palm, the source of the blood. Relief floods through me as I realise that the blood isn't hers. Where the fuck is Brotherton?

"With my blood, I mark you for my master." He parades among the flock, marking their foreheads. Blood bringing power, earthy and ancient, to this gathering. A thunderclap goes off in my head as I feel, a few miles, away a rift opening. Vincenzo, it appears, was right. A vision of the event sears into me. My body arching as if connected to electricity.

Another Altar, a small gathering and a different sacrifice. They have duped us. The real masters are not even here. They have completed the ritual and siphoned off the essence from here. The blackness of the rift sucks all light into it and I know It has crossed over. In a flash the image is gone. Leaving me gasping for air. Another dig with a heel and I lose my vision to tears of pain and impotent rage. Michelle is raised from the altar, alive and well but covered in his blood and marked for their master, who is on his way. She seems to be happy, the smile on her face is wide and beaming. She is the star turn. More so than Hannah. Young women are so competitive.

"Make your offering girl." His voice is thick with lust, and his body beginning to show that desire made flesh. "Our Master is coming. The world trembles at his footsteps." For once he is speaking the literal truth. I know that he is on his way, and we need help.

"My body is my offering.'" She speaks softly but in the expectant silence it sounds like a shout. I can feel the coming storm, like a tsunami charging across the flat sands. When it gets here and crashes over us, we are all well and truly screwed.

"Show us; be not ashamed of your beauty." Her dainty fingers untie the white robe letting it fall away and pool at her feet. She steps proudly forward for all those gathered to see. She has much to be proud of. A heavy crash as the portable ram bursts in the front doors. Brotherton has arrived before their master.

Chapter 36

God must love a western. I wanted rescued much earlier but in the nick of time will have to do. The stamping of heavy feet and manly shouts are like the sweetest hymns ever sung. The black uniformed, body-armour wearing, night stick wielding shock troops fill the room. Brotherton is shouting and so are most of the storm troopers. Nut-kicker has given me a souvenir as he legs it. I retch, depositing my tossed cookies all over the floor. My misery is almost complete. Groggily I get to my hands and knees. I need to get up quickly. There is so little time. 'Breathe.' I tell myself. I can feel the rising tide. He is coming.

Brotherton is directing the traffic as cuffs are applied and the screaming half naked women are carried from the church to our row of police vans. I manage to cough out his name and catch his eye. He looks shocked but glad to see me I think. He covers the ground quickly and is solicitous of my health. Apparently I look like shit. Well looks aren't deceiving after all.

"There is no time Brotherton. We need to clear everyone out now." I must sound crazed as I cling on to him. I am unsteady on my feet and grab a pew with my other hand, anchoring me vertically.

"It's fine. We got them." Bless him, he has no idea. He seems to think we are about to close them down.

"Get her out." I point at the now covered and compliant Michelle Brookes. She is being comforted by a female officer. The lights are on and the place is in chaos. I need a drink; the taste of vomit is not my favourite. A tremor strikes the building. He is here.

"It is too late Brotherton. Get her behind us." His wide eyes tell me that he can feel it too. "Now!" I bark at him. "Move." And his limbs start to respond. We may be in deep trouble here. I step into the space between the pews directly between Michelle Brookes and the entrance. This may be a last bastion to slow the devil that is coming. Sort of like Verdun. 'Il ne passeront pas'. If it gets to Michelle, all marked in blood, then she will be lost and we will be lunch. Failure will be total and devastating.

The house of God, no matter which denomination, is a powerful place. The fact that this one has squatters has an effect but doesn't totally remove the sanctity. It is still His house. I hope that tonight at this Sabbat, and peak of Dark power, there is enough to drive away our enemy. Now is the time for faith, the flaw in my character. Knowledge is not faith, and it might matter this time.

"Brotherton, light that fucking candle." I point to the 'God is in' candle that they have extinguished. He looks nonplussed. "Just do it." I shout. I see him fumbling for his lighter. Michelle and the female police officer are in the far corner, ashen faced and afraid. They have no understanding of why they are afraid but they are right to be. We are in peril. Brotherton is all thumbs yet getting there.

"In the name of the Father, and of The Son and of The Holy Spirit. Amen. Blessed is he who comes in the name of The Lord. Hosannah in the highest." I cross myself and pull myself together. Raising my crucifix to my lips, a kiss of my saviour and I am ready. The cold of the Otherworld floods the church. The chill crawls across the floor and washes over everything it encounters. A synchronised scream fills the air from behind me. The air ripples. It is kick-off time.

A heavy thump, thump, thump builds the fear ahead of the arrival. The violent thrust of the doors wrenches them from their hinges with glass and splinters cascading around. The boom of the exterior doors slamming shut tells me there is no escape. Hairy, heavily-muscled, otherworldly arms extend from a huge hulking form, half hidden by the shadows. The cloven hooves I expect to see are reptilian, clawed and vicious looking. Not a goat manifestation then.

"I am come." A voice like nails on a blackboard assails our ears. I wonder if mine have started to bleed the spite so vicious and malice laden.

"You have no place here. Go back to the pit from whence you came." All formal and clear. Its never a good idea to get in front of a devil-demon thing but tonight I have no choice. Red baleful eyes turn on me. I feel my skin trying to crawl away as it stares. I want to run, and keep running, but there is nowhere to go. If I fail, we four will perish and that I cannot allow. It steps inside. I can feel its discomfort. Good, we might not get munched after all. The sanctity of a church is hard to erase and our visitor will not bear its touch without discomfort.

"You cannot withstand me. I come to claim my own." It hulks forward, talons looking mighty sharp and cruelly curved. The smell of rot is overpowering, and if I hadn't already tossed my cookies I would be joining in the synchronised vomiting with the others. Their retching bringing amusement to the Demon before me. Humans are so weak before him. "I am the master here." It spits the words from a, very unlikely, many fanged mouth. That mouth was designed for shredding flesh not massacring the spoken word.

"My Lord, is the Master here. His light shines bringing light to his house and the world." I hope Brotherton has managed to light the candle. While not really necessary, it is symbolic. Symbols are often forgotten or misunderstood but there is much that is ritual that has its roots in magic and the mystics of early

Christianity.

A buffeting wind howls through the church, carrying a cruel laugh with it, causing The draperies to flap wildly and causing the hanging lights to swing on their cables. All around the altar candles are extinguished by the blast. All but one, God is in the House; and right behind me. The tumbling padded kneelers careen across the floor like a snowstorm.

"In the Name of The Father, Son and Holy Spirit I abjure you. You shall return to the hells that were made for you. I abjure you in the Name of Christ. Go from here. Your time has passed." All very serious and laden with power. I feel it flinch before me. Words have such power and at times like this key phrases unlock real power.

Gobbets of half digested flesh and green ichors pours from its maw in a projectile stream, splattering around me and (no doubt) ruining another pair of shoes and trousers. The air is filled with the sweet stench of decay and saliva is filling my mouth, a precursor to my vomiting.

"I will feast!" it roars, and sadly I get the spray. Lead-lined stained-glass windows behind the altar shatter outwards under the percussive blast. I can hear screaming and hope it isn't me. There will be no way to hush this up; too many will be witnesses to this event.

"You will never pass. The Lord of Hosts is with me. His

power compels you. Begone. I abjure you in His name." I reach for the lead crystal vial in my pocket, which luckily survived the kicking I got. The Beast thrashes left and right, splintering pews and scattering the hand-embroidered padded-kneelers that had survived the earlier blast. A lovely thistle adorned one sails by. With an ear bursting roar it surges forward.

You know that faith I was talking about earlier. Now comes its test. My damnation and evisceration are dependent on my faith. The certain knowledge of the existence of the Almighty is not the question. The faith being tested is in his redeeming my soul, in His having washed away the Original Sin and in his divine love and protection.

"I will feast on your sin-laden soul. I smell the carnal sins, you are covered in them. I will savour their flavours over a very long time, your torment will last for eternity." A triumphal sneer accompanied these words, and a snatch at my chest. Grabbing a clawful of fabric the Beast hoists me from my feet towards the fangs.

The blistering swish of Holy water, criss-crossing at close range forced the Beast to recoil and cast me away. Glad as I am to be away from those teeth and the smell I am less glad to crash into the rail and crumple in an agonised heap. This time the synchronised screaming has me in the team. The bass section is supplied by our Otherworld visitor, holy water sizzling and searing putrid flesh. It seems to have gotten some in the eyes, which has got to smart some. The wild flailing of massive clawed limbs sends pews in all directions. Furniture piling and destruction for beginners.

I am helped to my feet by Brotherton who, bless him, still looks terrified. The hammering on the main doors outside are a mere counterpoint in the cacophony. We need to pray. It's a powerful weapon in fighting the enemy. I drop to my knees dragging Brotherton beside me.

"Pray. By all you hold dear, Pray!" I cough and a little froth escapes my lips. Worse still it is pink froth. Not the best sign at the moment. Breathing seems to be hard work and a bit gurgly.

"Our father, who art in heaven, hallowed be thy name." I start it off for him, maybe the female police officer will join in. Michelle is out of it, probably just as well. Brotherton is starting to mumble along and might even be getting some of the words right. The Beast is flailing and clawing the air as our words land heavily on it. They must feel like physical blows to the demon as it reels and sways beneath them.

"Keep going, it is working." I shout to Brotherton who is only three feet away. I stand and wielding my holy water, I advance. The roaring in my ears is getting louder and louder.

"With this Holy water, I cast you back into the pit. Like Saint Michael and his Angels did so long ago. With this Holy water I abjure you. Begone! I command you in the name of The Lord. He who is Lord of All. He who is with me and lends me his strength. I abjure you, Unclean Spirit. Go back to the Abyss and await your destruction." I manage to get the words out past the agony in my chest.

The Holy water drops bring a scream of torment as they land but it is running out, my words and Brotherton's prayer are heavy blows causing the Beast to flinch repeatedly. If I can drive it from this church, Michelle Brookes we will be safe this night. The alternative is not one to contemplate.

The last drops are gone and it is still here, screaming but still here. Fumbling in my pockets I feel the small ceramic jar of holy unction. It may be what I need. I hope so as we have not much else left. I feel cold and my fingers seem to be trembling. The cough erupting from my chest doubles me over. It seems that Beast and I are well and truly fucked. If there was a referee then this fight would have been stopped by now. The Holy unction has smeared all over my hand as I fumbled the lid and drop the jar. Worse than a butter-fingered slip catcher.

"You will be mine Nazarene." Snarls reach my ears. It is right next to me, the claws dig into my shoulders as it pulls me in for a kiss. I would scream but there is no air in me to do so. The agony so intense is ripping through me as the claws rend my flesh. I gulp for air like a landed, desperate fish. The snapping of my collarbone goes unnoticed under the searing pain of the claws gouging deeper. There isn't much left in me as I start to feel my life ebbing away under its claws.

"I abjure you." I manage a whisper as my unction smeared hand pushes against its sweat covered chest. I am too stubborn to give up and die. The blinding burst of white light and a close range detonation are all I am aware of. It is over, my lights are going out.

Chapter 37

Waking up on a hospital bed, with tubes coming out of me, is not a great habit to get into. I feel so heavy that I just wait, my eyes are as focussed as a Vaseline smeared lens. Soft focus, more like unable to focus but I hope that will improve. I do the check. I can move my toes. If nothing else that is a win. My tongue is thick and cardboard-like. I try my eyes again as I wiggle my toes but that seems too much for me, I have no energy. It feels like I am just empty; no fuel. My leaden eyelids resist my attempts to get them open properly. My ears are working fine. I can hear a button being pressed and a whispered 'He's wakening now' reaches me. I am awake, its not like I am dead. The footsteps seem quite hurried, clacking on the floor. The lights are so dim, must be part of the efficiency savings. Another budget saving for the national treasure that is the NHS.

"Father Steel, can you hear me?" A bright white light is shone right in my eye; oh that's nice. Thanks, not. My mouth is moving but not much is coming out. They fill my mouth with water, lukewarm plastic tasting and foul. It works though. Apparently very little can't be improved with a little lube.

"I can hear you." I manage to croak, "Now get that fucking light out of my eyes" I want to add but I manage to avoid saying so. There is an audible sigh of relief from my care team. It seems they were very worried about me.

"You are a very lucky man, Father Steel. That was a close call." He's doing his best to make me feel better. Aren't doctors getting younger these days? Add them to the list that includes policemen.

"Being that close to a gas explosion and surviving, basically intact, is a miracle." He whitters on. So we are calling it a gas explosion, oh aye that will work.

"You will be going for some tests, and I will see you in the morning. Rest now, you are in good hands. I will contact Inspector Brotherton and let him know you can see him in the morning." There, there now off to sleep. The drugs are great, I just let all his drivel wash by and not one sarcastic reply. Gas leak, for goodness sake. You couldn't make it up. I wonder what stellar genius thought up that excuse. It is worse than the dog ate my homework.

So Broken collarbone, broken ribs, punctured lung and severe lacerations to the shoulder counts for basically intact these days. Let's not add in the nut-ache and stamp mark on my head, the black eyes, split lip, stitches in my scalp and the bruising pretty much covering my body. Yeah I am a picture of health. I read my chart and the notes on the file that was left casually lying about, when I looked like I was sleeping. Bruising to the brain and swelling from a possible fractured skull also part of my pretty much intact. I hate to see what not intact looked like.

"Father." Brotherton, is standing at the foot of the bed. My grumpy, frowny face is in place until I realise it is him. I wasn't really focussing as I let my mind wander about in the sedated state.

"Brotherton, you made it too." I smile a little. I don't want to laugh as it will hurt like hell. He has not a mark on him. That is so unfair. How did he manage that?

"Gas explosions are so dangerous. I am glad you are still with us." I wince at the in joke. He can see what I think of the Gas leak. "Father, I have some updates for you. We got a good sweep of these guys. Organ trafficking money is being recovered and charges laid on a number of the group. As Hannah is sixteen there was no offence there as she consented but the drugging and coercion of a minor has a few more in the cells. They will be going to HM Peterhead with the sex offenders or Barlinnie for the general criminals.' He seems happy. He got his men. I manage a twitch of my lips, it looks like a smile sort of.

"Well done, Brotherton. Big promotion in the offing for you?" I try to be interested. We got some of them but not the leader nor his inner cabal. Still a win is a win, as they say.

"No chance, they are slimming down the upstairs posts anyway. I might be moving to a new unit anyway." He looks at me, it is a funny look. Fucked if I can be bothered to ask.

"Yes, it was real. Welcome to my world." I don't need to be psychic to know what he wanted to know. He knew the answer but just wanted me to say it. A little confirmation that he wasn't hallucinating.

"I'll bet the notebooks are very interesting reading." I wink and try to smile. How on earth are they going to keep that one quiet. Good luck with that.

Chapter 38

It's funny, waiting to go that is. It was bad enough being sent back to my home town to solve a murder but being reluctant to go now that my task is done is, somewhat, surprising. A definite touch of maudlin sentimentality. Who would have thought it? I am a cold, uncaring bastard I hear. It appears I will miss the place.

The replacement should be here soon. I hope he is prompt. I have completed the final walk rounds and tidy ups. The service of re-consecration has been completed, in private, and God's candle is proclaiming that the Big Man is in. I have cleansed the building from bottom to top and it is now, once again, the house of God. It is a shiny, clean spiritual haven. The building works were completed by the time I was fit to walk unaided and without the stick. The new guy wont be told everything, obviously, but I'll know. And that's enough. The Bishop, personally, recommends this guy, so that's him fucked then.

My little red sunny waits patiently to take me back to my salubrious digs in the Capital, commonly called the barracks. Actually it is the very well appointed seminary. Spartan might be the best description but as I have very little, what do I actually need? An e-book reader would be nice, a Porsche perhaps? Maybe if there was a performance bonus scheme?

A blue Volvo pulls into the car park, with a young-ish, dog-collared, chap behind the wheel. Aren't Priests getting younger these days? Must be an age thing. He hasn't noticed my lurking and he seems genuinely cheerful. I am sure that won't last. I've met the congregation. I wonder if Angela will tempt and corrupt him? A little smile turns up the corner of my mouth, I hope she's over that little kink. I have had a tearful meeting with her and we have managed to get help for Michelle in the form of a scholarship summer school where she will be 'helped'. I hope she doesn't need excoriated. David Brookes just thinks he is surrounded by moody women and no one will tell him otherwise.

He parks and makes his way towards me and when I step from the shadow I catch him a little by surprise. That's me the ninja-master. Much like David Carradine's Kung Fu.

"Father Steel?" His hand extends and a smile that goes from perfect white teeth tips to his sparkly blue eyes. A real smile with nothing held back. Shiny.

"Good to meet you Father Matthew, I'm sure you'll be happy here." I do try occasionally. He doesn't need to know how clean I have made his new building.

"I am sure I shall. What are the congregation like? Are they recovered from the death of Father MacPhail?" His question hangs a little as I decide which version of events to share. Better not share too much.

"They take some getting used to. Although it is amazing what you can get used to. I think they need a new hand to take them forward." I smile, well more a sardonic twitch of my lips but it's the best I can do. A dossier has been left for his bedtime reading. It's a page turner. Perhaps I should have left a bottle of Johnny Walker to help him get over the shock. Too late, now.

"Excellent." We look at each other, he looks like a Priest whereas I just look a bit crumpled. I hand him the keys to his little part of the Rock of Saint Peter. Symbolic but he is impervious, perhaps it would be better if he stayed that way.

"Right, I'm off. Good luck Brother." I shake his hand again and he nods, still smiling. Clunk-kitty-clunk and the doors to my escape pod are unlocked. A quick pre-flight check and I pull away, the scream of the fan-belt setting my teeth on edge. Better get that fixed.

The End.

Father Steel continues his fight against the forces of Evil in 'In the Shadow of St Giles' as something stalks the streets of Edinburgh.

Printed in Great Britain
by Amazon